PUT ON
MY CROWN

Books by Betty Levin

The Beast on the Brink
A Binding Spell
The Keeping-Room
Landfall
The Zoo Conspiracy

PUT ON MY CROWN

by Betty Levin 🦋

LODESTAR BOOKS E. P. DUTTON • NEW YORK

Copyright © 1985 by Betty Levin

All rights reserved. No part of this publication may be
reproduced or transmitted in any form or by any means,
electronic or mechanical, including photocopy, recording,
or any information storage and retrieval system now
known or to be invented, without permission in writing
from the publisher, except by a reviewer who wishes to
quote brief passages in connection with a review written
for inclusion in a magazine, newspaper, or broadcast.

Library of Congress Cataloging in Publication Data

Levin, Betty.
  Put on my crown.
  Summary: Cast ashore on a bleak island, survivors
of a shipwreck find the islanders' treatment of them
kind, yet strange and a little frightening.
  [1. Shipwrecks—Fiction] I. Title.
PZ7.L5759Pu 1985 [Fic] 84-28845
ISBN 0-525-67163-3

Published in the United States by E. P. Dutton, Inc.,
2 Park Avenue, New York, N.Y. 10016

Published simultaneously in Canada by
Fitzhenry & Whiteside Limited, Toronto

Editor: Virginia Buckley   Designer: Edith T. Weinberg

Printed in the U.S.A.   COBE   First Edition
10 9 8 7 6 5 4 3 2 1

for Bara
and for Jane and Bill

one 🐉

At first Vinnie did her best to distract the children. But the tiny cabin, despite the shelves and cubbies so like a toy house, had lost its charm for them. It had a place for everything, yet room for nothing.

As the storm rose, so did Joel's excitement. He kept opening the cabin door to peek out into the saloon. Vinnie couldn't blame him. The saloon seemed to them a world apart from the rest of the ship. There the velvet draperies, the crystal chandelier, and mirrored wall made you think of a throne room. It was always fun to watch the grown-up passengers strolling or dining amid all that elegance. Only now they clutched at any solid object they could grasp, and at some objects that weren't solid enough. Joel stared, riveted.

Vinnie understood how he felt. When the ship reared and plunged, she thrilled to it too. And there was an edge to her excitement, almost like recognition, as though she were reliving a voyage from out of the past. Probably she was—a voyage she must have read about and then forgotten, an adventure at sea. There was a difference, though. In storybooks, the storm-tossed ships were usually grand sailing vessels, not lumbering hulks like the *Roger F. Laing*, with its patched bow and its deck layered with soot from the blackened smokestack. All the same, there was something stirring in the reek of slimy lines, in the true curve of lifeboats lashed to rusted rings, and in the churning water far below.

Grace pressed close to Joel. The cabin door opened a little more. Then the ship rolled mightily. Vinnie scrambled to keep the door from flipping the children backward. She caught sight of a lady who seized the edge of a table and pitched sideways with the cloth in her hands. Platters and a vase crashed to the floor. So did the lady.

Joel clutched at Grace. "Look!" he commanded, his eyes wide. "Did you see that?"

People rushed to the lady's assistance, but Grace had fixed her gaze on the crystal chandelier swinging overhead. "It's going to fall," she said. "And do you know what I'm going to do, Vinnie? I'm going to pick up one of those glass pieces with all the colors in it. Will they let me keep it?"

"No, Grace. It's part of the ship. It belongs to the *Roger F. Laing.*"

"But we could ask. You could, Vinnie. You could very politely ask the captain for me."

Vinnie shook her head. "A nursery maid doesn't speak to the captain."

"Then ask Mr. Powdermaker to ask. There he is now. Ask him before the glass falls and is swept away."

Mr. Powdermaker, whose long, bendy legs reminded Vinnie of a fly's, picked his way among the staggering passengers. He offered his arm to another lady on the verge of falling.

"Mr. Powdermaker can't be bothered about trifles. Besides, that chandelier won't fall. The *Roger F. Laing* is a safe ship. Mr. Powdermaker assured your mother it was, and he knows all about such things."

"Is Mother's ship safe too?"

"Of course. She chose it, so it must be."

"It has a better name than ours. *North Sea Queen* sounds grand."

Vinnie thought so too, but she said, "Never mind that. Be glad of the *Roger F. Laing,* because if it weren't for this ship, we should have had to stay behind. And be glad of Mr. Powdermaker too, that he was willing to take Master Perry in his cabin. At least you have your big brother on board."

"I wish it was Mother instead," Grace said.

"Well, it couldn't be helped, could it? Just think how lucky it was that Mr. Powdermaker was there to help us when your mother found out only one cabin had been booked on the *North Sea Queen.* At least we're on our way to North America, and we have Mr. Powdermaker and Master Perry with us."

"And your cousin Lottie too," Grace reminded her.

"That's right. And all those children from Miss Covington's school."

Joel turned to her. "I haven't seen them since the first day. Where are they?"

"'Tween decks," Vinnie told him. "Another part of the ship." She knew that neither Grace nor Joel had glimpsed the steerage quarters as she had. She wouldn't tell them about the rows of bare bed shelves like wooden stalls, the din, and the darkness.

"Couldn't we visit them?" Grace wanted to know.

Later, after the storm, Vinnie would have to explain that steerage passengers were not allowed to mingle with those in cabins and staterooms. For now she just said, "Look what trouble people are having trying to cross the saloon. We must take care. We mustn't add to the trouble."

"I could get across that floor without any trouble," Joel insisted.

"Well, you're not going anywhere," Vinnie told him. "Not till the storm goes away."

"I want to see the waves," Joel said. "I want to see them splashing on everything."

"Come and sit down, and we'll play a game."

3

"There's no room for a game in here," he complained.

"Come and sit down." Vinnie shut the door.

"Maybe it's teatime," Joel suggested. "Maybe," he added hopefully, "they'll bring us jam with our bread."

Vinnie had no idea how long the storm might last. The children had eaten nothing since breakfast. It had been dark outside for hours, but maybe that was because of the storm. What if it raged all through the night? How would she get meals for Grace and Joel? She had promised Mrs. Stott to attend to all their needs.

Vinnie took Joel by his shoulders and made him look into her eyes and promise not to try to find the steerage children while she went to fetch something for tea.

"Won't the man bring it?" Grace asked.

"I expect all the men are needed in the storm. Grace, while I'm gone, I don't want you to stir. Joel, do you understand what I've just told your sister?"

Joel nodded. "Will you bring gooseberry jam?"

"I'll bring whatever I can," Vinnie informed him as she stepped into the saloon and pulled the door shut.

The passengers were retreating to their cabins. Vinnie watched to see how they managed. She doubted she could carry anything bulky or slippery with the floor tilting this way and that. Clutching the slant bar fixed to the wall, she saw the children's older brother clinging to a bar just like hers across the saloon. He caught her glance and scowled. She supposed he didn't like her to see him stuck like that. Why mind, she wondered, when everyone was in the same boat? *In the same boat* made her laugh. Master Perry glared at her. He must think she was laughing at *him*. Quickly she set off. Too quickly. She stumbled into a bench and was thrown to her knees. That would make Master Perry feel better, she thought. Then she stopped thinking about him. She had to concentrate on keeping her balance so that she could gain the passageway beyond the saloon.

But it was hopeless there. Things crashed all about her. People

4

fell, and others, stooping to help them, went sprawling as well. The wind's shrieking filled the corridor; yet it seemed to Vinnie that human cries pierced the wind and the wood and the iron. Where did they come from? She clutched the wall to keep herself upright. Someone quite near yelped—a sudden shout of surprise and pain. Maybe Vinnie had imagined the other cries; anyway, they weren't right here where people were struggling and seeking places of safety. The only thing to do was turn back while she could. It was more important to see the Stott children safe on their sleeping shelves than to fetch them bread and jam.

A tide of people thrust Vinnie back. Then she broke through. There was a new commotion in the saloon. Had someone been injured? The ship heeled sideways and threw her to the floor. When she regained her footing, she found Mr. Powdermaker at the center of the commotion, Joel under his arm, Perry beside them.

"Joel!" she cried seeing that the boy was drenched. "What happened? Are you all right?"

Perry whipped around. "No thanks to you. He tried to go out on deck. My parents will hear about this."

Mr. Powdermaker waved a dismissal. "Oh, come now. There never was such a child for getting into scrapes."

Vinnie's heart raced. "Where's Grace?" she asked Joel.

"In there." Joel pointed to the cabin. "You made her promise not to stir."

"I meant you as well. You must know that." She took Joel from Mr. Powdermaker. "I'll get you dry now before you catch cold."

"I'm not cold," he said in his funny, deep voice. But his clothes were clinging to him, and he was beginning to shiver.

Perry said, "Vinnie is here to prevent scrapes like this, not to go off and leave the children."

"She went to get bread and jam for tea," Joel told him.

"Did she? I don't see any."

Vinnie clamped her mouth tight. Master Perry was always

looking for faults in her. The trouble was, this time he was right. She should never have left the two little ones.

Mr. Powdermaker said, "Things will likely get worse for a while. I doubt anyone will be fetching tea. Vinnie made a small mistake, that's all, and Joel was disobedient and naughty. I don't think I need to remind you," Mr. Powdermaker added, "that Vinnie has cared for Joel and Grace for nearly two years, and well enough for your mother to entrust them to her care on this voyage. And Joel owes his life to Vinnie."

"I scarcely need reminding, sir. I've heard of it often enough. The happy accident."

Vinnie could feel the blood rush to her cheeks. She turned Joel around to the cabin door.

"You can't trade on that accident for the rest of your days," Perry called to her back. "You'd better watch your step, Miss Highness."

Mr. Powdermaker laughed. "Thank goodness there are no highnesses where I come from. Now, I hope you two are not going to quarrel like children in the middle of a storm at sea."

"Well, she is a child," Perry mumbled. "She's only just fourteen."

"And you act like one," Vinnie returned under her breath.

"So am I a child," Joel declared. "I'm the smallest child, but my shoes are bigger than Grace's."

Except, thought Vinnie, as she stripped off his wet clothes, except for all those littler ones between decks in steerage. Except for the bundled babies carried aboard, and the children clutching cups and loaves and the skirts of someone leading them down into those dismal quarters where they would remain for the entire voyage across the Atlantic Ocean.

She couldn't rid herself of the thought that those muffled cries she'd heard came from steerage. What if one of them was Lottie calling her? Oh, that look Lottie had flung her way. It was just after boarding, when Lottie realized where she must go. Herded past the cabins toward the steep flight of stairs, Lottie had swiveled for an instant, her eyes blazing. Vinnie had tried to run after her. Miss Covington was urging the children on, lest they be separated, lest the doors closed before they were safely below. Steerage passengers clawed past Vinnie, dragging children and bundles and sending them down into the belly of the ship.

Vinnie had stared after them in disbelief. If only she could persuade Mr. Powdermaker to let Cousin Lottie remain with her and Grace and Joel. But there wasn't time. The door was closing; Grace and Joel needed her. Besides, there was the baggage to see to, for Mrs. Stott had warned that with the last-minute change of plans, the boxes and chests could easily be left on the docks.

But Lottie wasn't abandoned, Vinnie told herself as she rubbed Joel dry. Steerage couldn't be as cramped and ugly as it had appeared in that single glance, or Miss Covington would never have gone there. No, Lottie was not abandoned. On the contrary, she was one of a fortunate few, chosen and prepared for a whole new life in North America.

"Talk!" Joel commanded. "Vinnie, talk to me."

"My father was a sailor," Vinnie chanted, Joel bouncing on her lap, "he sailed across the sea. . . ." Joel chortled as the ship flung him high. "And all the fish that he could catch," Vinnie recited, catching Joel in her arms, "was one," with a bounce, "two," with another bounce, "*three!*" Here she let him almost drop.

"My turn, my turn," Grace shouted, and then doubled over and was sick.

After Vinnie had cleaned up Grace and dressed Joel in his brown poplin second best, they tried playing The Sea Is Rough. Vinnie, the Sea, pretended to forget which fish Joel was and which one Grace; but the cabin was too small for the game, and the storm pitched them so violently they had to scramble onto the lower sleeping shelf.

They sat clinging to the bedclothes until the storm entered a lull. Then Joel asked why Perry had been so cross with Vinnie.

"I expect he was worried," she answered. "You must never go on deck alone."

"You might have been swept into the sea," Grace scolded. "And drowned."

Joel shook his head. "Vinnie would fetch me out."

"It would be too late. It's not like falling off the wall."

The ship lurched and was slammed broadside. Vinnie grabbed the children. They listened to the water hissing across the deck.

"Ooh!" breathed Joel. "That must be the biggest wave in the world."

Grace clutched her stomach and moaned.

"Tell about the wall," Joel said to Vinnie. "It's my best story."

Vinnie could hear shouts outside their door. She wanted to open it, but she didn't dare let go of the children. "The wall," she repeated, her mind on the storm.

"Nurse was napping beside the wall," Grace prompted. She nestled against Vinnie. "Joel and I went marching. Nurse was always having naps and not noticing."

Joel stirred. "Why didn't Mother notice?"

"She was busy with Mr. Powdermaker," Vinnie explained. "Making plans, I suppose. They stopped to look at the children working in the turnip field."

"And there you were!" declared Grace.

"But they didn't know me. I was just one of the turnip pickers."

Joel pulled away and regarded her solemnly. "How didn't they know you if you were there?"

"Oh, Joel." Vinnie didn't want to go on. "Wouldn't you rather a story out of my book of Greek heroes? You know this one so well."

"Tell it anyway. Tell me again. Talk."

Vinnie tucked both children under the bedclothes and groped

8

for a handhold. Her stomach clenched like a fist. She made herself go on about her first meeting with the Stott family—how the turnip sack snagged on a stone and all the turnips tumbled out so that she had to stop to gather them up.

"Just think," Grace put in, "if the turnips hadn't spilled, Joel, you would have broken your head."

"Oh, I'm not sure," Vinnie began, but Joel was taken with the notion of a broken head.

"Could Father fix it? He put back Grace's doll's arm." Joel paused. "Only it came off again."

"Tell about Nurse screaming," Grace reminded Vinnie.

"Yes, well, she screamed when you went back to show her where Joel had got to."

"We were playing King of the Castle."

"Was I king?" Joel asked.

"After Grace left you, when you turned the corner and marched along the wall. That was when I started running. I could see how the ground fell away. The turnip field went down and down."

"I wasn't scared, though."

"You don't even remember," Grace told him.

"I'd remember if I was scared."

"Well, Nurse was," Vinnie put in. "When she saw where you were heading, she screamed." Vinnie shivered. Suddenly it was horribly vivid, the baby boy on the high wall, and the way her cramped body refused to straighten after hours on her hands and knees, pulling turnips and filling her sacks. She had stumbled across the deep furrows, her arms dangling, her hands raw and nearly frozen.

"Go on," prompted Joel. "Now comes the best part."

"When Nurse screamed, I saw you spin around. Your arms flew up. I thought you were waving." Even now she could see the little boy clutching at the empty air. How did she reach him in time?

9

How had she managed to wrench herself upright and fling herself in his way as he came hurtling down? She remembered only landing flat on her back with the wind knocked out of her.

"But you weren't waving," Grace told Joel. "You were falling. And Vinnie flew to your rescue. Flew on angel's wings. Isn't that right, Vinnie?"

"I was just there. I was able to."

"Mother says you were an angel from heaven. That's why she couldn't let you go back to the turnip field."

"I couldn't go back because my shoulder was hurt. I was under Joel and I'd struck a rock."

"You were brave. You let Joel play Horsey on you till Mother came."

"So she took you home," Joel declared. "Mr. Powdermaker wrapped you up in the carriage robe. But what happened to Nurse?"

"You know," Vinnie said.

"She was dismissed," Grace told him. "And Mother took on Vinnie because she had good manners and could read and write. Because she was deserving."

Joel tried to sit up. "And now will she be dismissed like Nurse?"

Vinnie pressed him back. "Not if you stay out of trouble."

"How can Joel stay out of trouble?" Grace wanted to know. "How can he, when our whole ship is in trouble?"

"And the sea," cried Joel. "The sea is rough and in trouble too."

Vinnie was thrown back. Outside their cabin something crashed. She would have to tie the children to the bed shelf. "Joel will be so good," she declared, tugging and knotting the linen, "he will be such a help that Master Perry will tell what a hero he was, and then your parents will be proud and not cross. And now you must pretend that you have had your tea and go to sleep. You must say your prayers. And don't forget your mother and father

10

and baby sister, or Master Perry and Mr. Powdermaker and . . . and all the people on this ship."

Grace tried to hug her, but Vinnie pressed the child's arms to her sides to bind her to the bed.

"Must we pray for Perry?" Joel asked. "He was mean."

"Especially for Perry," Vinnie answered.

"To make him nicer," Grace said.

"I'll pray for the other children too," Joel confided, "the ones somewhere else on the ship."

Vinnie nodded, but Grace said, "They don't need too much praying, for they are already lucky. Mother said they are the first of the poor children to be chosen. Their futures are full of promise. I think that's what she said."

"Ssh," whispered Vinnie, her stomach churning. Oh, please, let me not be ill, she prayed fervently.

"I can't sleep," Joel announced. "I just did sleep. I want to get up."

Vinnie didn't even answer him. By now the storm was raging so fiercely that all she could do was hold on to the children with all her might. She had no sense of time. There was an eternity of slamming. Then the whole ship stopped before it shuddered and plummeted into troughs that seemed as deep as the sea itself. The little cabinet door flew open, the pitcher and bowl tossed about. It took ages for them to break, and still the pieces were hurled and shattered some more. Vinnie covered the children's faces with her arms.

The porthole showed a gray wall—though whether of water or sky, Vinnie couldn't tell. Watching it made her stomach heave, so she faced down instead. Someone had been sick again. Joel? Grace? It could even have been herself. There was no way of cleaning up now.

two 🐙

Later, much later, the storm moved on. It left the ship floundering on mountainous waves, but the howling wind was gone. Now Vinnie could hear shouts and cries and running footsteps and things dragged across the saloon floor or rolling on the deck.

It's over, she thought. We're all right. Then she flushed, because she had meant by *we,* the two children and herself, not Lottie and the others below.

Grace opened her eyes. "Taste," she murmured. "Taste bad." Tears coursed down her cheeks and soaked the hair already plastered to her skin.

Vinnie said, "You'll feel better soon."

Still weeping, Grace closed her eyes, sighed, and slept.

It was dully light when Joel stirred. He didn't wake completely. He seemed not to recognize Vinnie. It was as if he preferred to see nothing.

The ship kept wallowing for all the daylight hours and well into the night. No one came to the cabin, but the children were too sick to care. Now the voices outside sounded almost normal. Work of some kind went on about the ship, even though it was dark, even though the ship itself was going nowhere.

Finally Grace began to call for her mother. Vinnie held her. "Poor little thing," she murmured, her eyes closing.

"Mother," whimpered Grace, and deep inside Vinnie a small child whimpered too.

Vinnie knew she was dreaming, because she was herself and yet not herself. Her short legs straddled the coaming to keep her balance. "Mama?" Mama wasn't there. Small Vinnie knew that Mama was lying on a narrow sleeping shelf—not asleep, but flopping from side to side like a fish on a table. "Mama," whimpered small Vinnie, and strangers answered. "Poor little thing," she heard, "with your mama brought to bed. Who's tending you then?" A kind lady gave her a muff to warm her hands in, a pretty fur muff to take her mind off her misfortune. It was softer than soft when she dipped her face into it.

She woke with her face pressed to the back of Joel's neck, his soft, thick hair against her skin. Dazed, she had to come out of the small Vinnie. The dream must have mixed her up with Grace. That was it. She had dreamed herself a child like Grace. Now it was morning again. Vinnie propped herself up on her elbow. Morning, and the sea felt calm. But the *Roger F. Laing* listed like a wounded whale.

Bleak and wan, the children began to pick themselves up. They were stiff. They ached all over. Then, suddenly, they became irritable and quarreled in fits and starts. They didn't ask about Perry or for food. They didn't mention their mother. They must be waiting to be delivered, Vinnie decided. Like her, they wanted only solid, dry land.

The cabin reeked. It needed airing and scrubbing, but there wasn't any water. Climbing uphill on the steeply sloping floor, Vinnie opened the door a crack and peeped out. A few people were about, mostly maids and ship's servants. Well, she was a maid; she had two young children to see to. She whispered to Grace to keep Joel inside with her, then slipped into the saloon.

13

It was transformed. The tables were tipped up and pushed to the wall. The great mirror was a craze of splinters. Nothing remained of the chandelier but the chain hanging slack from the ceiling. Everything was eerily quiet.

Vinnie made her way through the narrow, slanting corridor to the ship's kitchen. It was comforting to hear voices and the clatter of pans. She stood behind two other maids waiting for soup and biscuits to bring to their masters and mistresses.

"It's that cargo done it," the cook was saying. "Them railway irons breaking through."

"The steward said we won't go nowhere till the iron's put right," said one of the maids. "And the dead put in the sea."

"Dead!" Vinnie cried. "People died?"

The cook nodded. "At least two crew overboard, one killed on deck, and some in steerage." The ladle was poised over Vinnie's bowl. "How many you serving?"

"Three. How can I find out about the steerage passengers?"

"You can't. Door's bolted. Otherwise they'd be swarming all over." The cook slopped another ladleful into the big bowl. "Now watch how you carry that or you'll burn yourself."

Vinnie held the bowl away from her. "Is it very bad then?"

"Bad enough. Some of the gentleman passengers manned the pumps all night so the crew could patch the hole."

"Scare her," warned a maid, "and you'll start a regular panic."

"You mean," Vinnie persisted, "water through a hole? In steerage? What about the people there?"

"Oh, they're all right if they keep to those racks. There's high-up places for them to be. And the pump is going all the time."

"But you said some people died there."

"That was during the storm." The cook nodded to newcomers. "Make room now."

Vinnie stepped aside. "Can I go there? 'Tween decks?"

14

"You just carry that soup. Don't expect me to fill you up again if it spills."

Vinnie moved on. She had forgotten the biscuits, but she didn't dare set the bowl down now. Someone jostled her as she stepped into the saloon and then snarled at her for dripping soup on his shoes. He stumbled over to the draperies to wipe his shoes with the golden tassels that roped back the green velvet folds.

Clutching the bowl in one arm, Vinnie fumbled with the latch to the cabin door. It swung in so suddenly on the downward slope that Vinnie lurched forward. Then she stopped in her tracks. The tiny cabin was packed with children. Some were with Grace and Joel on the lower sleeping shelf. Others were on the upper shelf and on the floor against the cabinet.

Vinnie felt a trickle of warm soup along her wrist. She set the bowl at her feet. Several children leaned toward it. No one spoke.

Finally Cousin Lottie, perched on the travel box with a small child on her knees, said, "They'll catch us if you don't shut that door. They'll send us back."

Vinnie pushed the door uphill until it clicked closed. She went on staring at the children, all of them soaked and covered with filth.

Grace, her arm around the smallest child, said, "Let me feed this one, Vinnie. Isn't she beautiful?"

Vinnie saw only a pinched face, huge eyes, limp hands. Like a doll, the child registered nothing.

"Yes," Lottie declared briskly, "Nell first. She's the worst off."

They spooned soup into the child, coaxing her to swallow. When Vinnie started to wipe up what dribbled out the side of the child's mouth, Lottie grabbed the spoon and scraped up the drippings. "We're hungry," she snapped. "Don't you waste a drop."

Finally Nell began to suck at the spoon. Like a nursing baby, she sucked the broth, but turned her head away from the meat and potatoes.

After Vinnie portioned out the rest of the soup among the remaining children, she turned to Lottie. How had she managed to bring these children to the cabin?

"I had to. Miss Covington . . . Something's happened to her." Lottie's eyes filled with tears. "It was awful. We couldn't see, and I couldn't find the others. Everyone was screaming. They pushed and nearly knocked us down. It got to smelling so bad you couldn't breathe. I had Nell and the twins. I had to get out. Willie and Jack were with us. And Toby. He helped me boost them up when they opened the skylight. So he had to come too, and, oh, I'd have taken more, any of them, but they weren't there and someone was coming. We had to run."

"We was way high on the shelf," one of the boys explained. "We climbed through. We hid. Then Lottie took us here."

"Will they make us go back?" asked another boy. "Please, miss, don't let them."

"I can't hide the lot of you," Vinnie told them.

"I'll keep Nell," said Grace. "Can I dress her in something else?"

Vinnie glanced at Nell, who was beginning to shiver. If only Mrs. Stott were here. She would take these children in hand and sort them out. But Mrs. Stott was on the *North Sea Queen.* Perhaps she too was recovering from the storm and seeing to the baby and others.

Vinnie wrapped the steerage children in sheets and blankets and the old cloak that Mrs. Stott had made Vinnie take along even though it was far too big for her. "You never know," Mrs. Stott had insisted, and already she was proved right. The cloak might keep three children warm while Vinnie found some way to wash their soiled clothes.

"We'll start with the girls," Vinnie declared. "Lottie, you take the boys to the saloon and wait with them."

16

Lottie started to protest, but Vinnie simply marched them out herself and sat them on the bench at the far end of the saloon. She didn't think anyone would bother with them. The crew was cleaning up debris; the passengers were beginning to move up to the tilted deck. Maids sought food and clean bedding and water. Who would notice four boys and a girl sitting quietly on a bench?

Turning back to the cabin, Vinnie nearly stumbled into a seaman carrying a copper of water.

"Careful," he grumbled. "Bad enough fetching water like a cabin boy without no dumping."

"Sorry. Can I help?" Vinnie offered.

"It's for . . . let me see, I think they said Beckwith. Hope it's not much farther."

"Well, it can be for the Stotts, and then you're already there, no mistake." She opened the cabin door, nodding approval as he set the copper down. "That's fine then, and now you're done." She all but slammed the door after him.

Grace helped with buttons and shoes as Vinnie peeled off the girls' soiled clothes. One of the twins wept silently, afraid she would lose her dress. Without it, she couldn't stay in America. "Canada," corrected her sister. "It's our dresses for Canada."

"You'll have the dresses back all clean," Vinnie promised the children while she tried to scrub some life into them, "smocks and all." But she had to take care, because each child was covered with scrapes and bruises. Tucking Mrs. Stott's cloak around them, she put them to bed on the lower sleeping shelf.

She found Lottie and the boys just where she had left them; she sent Lottie and Joel for some proper food. "Tell them it's for the Stotts. They're supposed to send in our meals. Tell them."

She worked on the three steerage boys until they were clean and bound in sheets on the bed above the girls. After that, she dumped the clothes into the copper with a bit of soap, washed and wrung them as best she could, and set them in a heap on the cabinet. As soon as Lottie and Joel got back, she would look for a place to hang the clothes to dry.

She seemed to wait forever. When a knock came, she leaped up, then cautiously opened the door, leaning against it to keep it from swinging wide. There stood Mr. Powdermaker and Master Perry. Her heart sank. Mr. Powdermaker beckoned her into the saloon. Thank goodness he didn't want to come inside the cabin. She slipped out and pulled the door shut.

"There is bad news," he said.

Holding her breath, Vinnie gazed up at him.

"I'm afraid . . ." He stopped to cough. "There have been some casualties." Vinnie's gaze didn't waver. "Three unfortunate passengers, all adults, have been carried to the deck. I'm afraid one of them is Matron in steerage, Miss Covington. I don't yet know what has become of the children. There will be a service on deck later."

Vinnie said, "Some of the children are here. My cousin brought them."

"Did she! Upon my soul! Where?"

Vinnie nodded toward the cabin. "I've just bathed them. They were dreadfully dirty and soaked to the skin."

"Those Ragged School children in there?" exclaimed Perry. Opening the door, he nearly fell over the copper.

Grace, her finger to her lips, stood facing her older brother. "Perry," she whispered, "you must hush or leave."

Mr. Powdermaker dragged the copper with its remaining water out to the saloon. The heap of washed clothing tumbled from the cabinet onto the floor. Grace scowled warningly and pointed to the sleeping shelves. The three girls were stretched out—the twins wrapped in each other's arms, Nell apart, her blue-veined eyelids fluttering like moths. The three boys on the upper shelf were propped up as though sitting, but they were sound asleep. The bruises on their heads and shoulders were livid against the sheet.

18

"One is Jack," Grace informed them in a whisper, "and the other is Willie, but I don't know which is which. The big one's Toby."

"What are you going to do with them?" Perry demanded of Mr. Powdermaker.

"Let them sleep," Mr. Powdermaker replied in a low voice.

"And these are Amy and Mabelle Tucker, and the little one's Nell Haskins. She's my special one."

"I mean," Perry added stiffly, "when their clothes are dry."

"They'll attend the service. And then . . ."

"Then?" whispered Vinnie.

"Then we'll see. We must see about the others too. We can't do much about that until we're under way again. The first order of ship business just now is with the railway irons. No one is available for anything else until they find a way to fasten that cargo."

Hearing Joel's deep voice at the door, Vinnie quickly opened it. "Careful, we're all crowded in here," she warned, letting Lottie know they weren't alone. Lottie handed in a tray with buns, a pot of tea, and three mugs. There was also a dish of cheese and cold meat.

"Ah," declared Mr. Powdermaker, "a feast." He backed out to make room.

Perry stared at Vinnie. "If you're going to take those wet things out of here, you can fetch a tray for us too on your way back."

"That would be a help," Mr. Powdermaker told her. "We're famished, Perry and I. We'll wait in our cabin."

By now Vinnie was so hungry, she could have gobbled all the buns herself. She took one and ate it slowly and drank a mug of tea. She left the rest for Lottie to hand out. She didn't have to worry about how it would be divided. Lottie was fiercely fair-minded.

She found a kind of scullery where she could hang the clothes. A man with a broom tried to set her to work there, but she ducked away and took her place at a table where each servant was handed a kettle of steamed pudding. Two kettles, she demanded; she was serving two cabins. On her way back, people tried to wrest the kettles from her. "Be careful," she warned, "they're hot." One maid did grab hold, but with a cry, let go again. "There," Vinnie told her, "didn't I say?" She hurried on to the cabin.

"Oh," breathed Lottie, "it does smell good! Is that what you dined on in the saloon?"

Vinnie ladled pudding into the empty tea mugs. What good would it do to tell Lottie of feasts they had not tasted? Vinnie and Grace and Joel had peeked at roasts and dressed fowl carried into the saloon, at the fruit compotes and pasties brought to each dining table. One kind steward had brought them apricot preserves and gooseberry jam with their tea and bread and porridge; that had been their best meal. So the steamed pudding, thick and heavy with suet and dried fruit, was almost as much of a treat for them as for Lottie and the others. It brought a touch of color to some of the exhausted children. Only Nell turned away from it and sank into a listless stupor.

After settling the children again, Vinnie carried the remaining pudding across the saloon to Mr. Powdermaker and Perry. Perry looked in the kettle. "Not even full," he complained.

"There were no full servings," Vinnie told him.

"Had you anything for the children?" Mr. Powdermaker asked her.

Vinnie flushed. "Yes, sir. Thank you."

"*Our* dinner, no doubt," Perry remarked.

"There's enough here. Vinnie, you'll have to take care of the little ones."

"Yes, sir."

"He means your charges, my brother and sister."

"I mean all of the children. They and Miss Covington were brought here through your mother's arrangements. I'm quite sure Vinnie understands what must be done for the present."

20

"For the present," Perry muttered. "Then back they go, those Ragged School children. Where they belong. As soon as ever they can."

Vinnie spoke to Mr. Powdermaker. "I expect they'll sleep awhile. They'll be no trouble. I've set their clothes to dry."

In the saloon Vinnie overheard talk about the shifting cargo. Passengers wondered whether the ship would have to return to Liverpool instead of continuing on across the Atlantic. Someone remarked that there ought to be an adjustment in fares. The voices rose and fell. Vinnie could hardly distinguish them anymore.

The cabin was dim and quiet. Even Lottie had jammed herself into bed with the others and was sound asleep. Vinnie sank onto the floor and leaned her head against the mattress. She let her eyes rove from one child to the next. Mrs. Stott's arrangements. The children were here because of Mrs. Stott's grand scheme to prepare them—not only for service, but for the lives they would live when that service was completed. She had consulted Mr. Powdermaker again and again, and listened to his opinion of his American clients, who looked for strength and diligence in the children they took, not education. But Mrs. Stott went right ahead with her scheme.

Where was Mrs. Stott now? Had the *North Sea Queen* missed this storm? Here were some of the first children setting forth according to plan; they had no matron now—they had no one.

Somehow Vinnie would have to manage for them until they landed safely, until Mrs. Stott could carry on with her arrangements.

three 🦎

Vinnie woke to a rapping on the door. Someone shouted a message from Mr. Powdermaker: "Come at once to the service on deck; bring the children."

The saloon was strangely empty. She glanced through the open door to the deck. Dense fog. Racing to the scullery, she snapped down the children's clothes and ran back to the cabin. Never had her fingers worked so fast. She propped up arms and pulled down sleeves and fastened hooks. Nell was so slow Vinnie considered leaving her to sleep some more, but something made her want to keep them all together. She grabbed Grace's *Infant's Magazine* and stuffed it inside Nell's bodice to protect her from the damp air. She snatched up Mrs. Stott's old cloak, tied a shawl over her own head and flung another at Lottie, then led the children up and out into the silent throng of passengers.

Vinnie could hardly see. Lottie tugged on her cloak and whispered, "There's a place for the little ones." The place was a pig crate. Ropes secured it to cables slanting away into the fog. No one was standing on its wooden roof, probably because of the pigs underneath it. One of them had lacerations on its neck and side.

Toby helped set the smaller children on top. Vinnie tried to

22

curve Nell's fingers around the rope, but the child wouldn't hold on. Lottie hoisted herself up and then swept her arms around Nell.

Vinnie told herself she should count the children, but she wasn't sure how many there were. Names, she thought, while up forward the captain's voice droned through the creak and rattle of deck lines. If only she could remember them all. She looked around. Where was Joel? In sudden panic, she called him softly, urgently. What if he'd wandered off again?

The biggest of the steerage boys touched her shoulder. "Miss," he said, "around the other side."

Vinnie circled the crate. There squatted Joel, his face only inches from a cracked, dry snout. She jerked him up by his arm, away from the hairy pig cheek pressed against the slats. "Stand up with the others," she whispered. "You must show your respect."

"Why?"

"Because the people lost their lives," she said. "They're heroes."

Now he was interested. "Who? What did they do?"

She thought of the crew members who had died. She had heard about an entire family, steerage passengers who were too late for entrance below and who had been allowed to shelter in a crude deckhouse meant for animals. Nothing remained of that shack; it was rumored that nothing remained of the family either. There would be prayers for them and for Miss Covington and for the others who were to be buried at sea.

"They fought the storm," she told him in a low voice, wondering suddenly whether they had gone to their deaths as heroes or, as she would have done, terrified and clinging to lifelines. "You must pray for them. Listen now. Hear the captain." She lifted Joel onto the crate.

" 'I am the resurrection, and the life,' " she heard the captain say.

"Where are they?" Joel asked, craning, unable to see. "Where are the heroes?"

Vinnie clambered onto the crate and raised Joel as high as she could. The crowd shifted to make way for crew members bearing sheeted bundles, which Vinnie knew to be the bodies of the dead.

" '. . . whosoever liveth and believeth in me,' " intoned the captain, his voice strained and hoarse, " 'shall never die.' " And the first sheeted body slid away.

From her perch on the pig crate, Vinnie could see no more. The splash seemed a long time coming; it was very small. A whole person, thought Vinnie, and hardly a splash at all.

The sea carried it off or down, Vinnie couldn't tell which, and while she pondered, another sheeted bundle was sent into the water. Miss Covington, she told herself, trying to feel something. She looked at the children. The littlest wore a look of absolute indifference. That's Nell, thought Vinnie, Nell Haskins. Probably she didn't understand what was happening. And of course the big boy was Toby. He was staring at the sailors who handled the plank; maybe he was thinking of pirate stories. The twins looked properly respectful, eyes ahead, hand in hand. Grace was trying to straighten her stocking where it wrinkled at her ankle. And Lottie was darting glances this way and that.

As the last bundled figure was raised onto the plank, it came to Vinnie that even in these few minutes the fog had thickened. Ghostliness attended the body wrapped in shadowy whiteness.

The captain's voice grated through the vapors. "Amen."

"Amen," responded the passengers and crew, joined and muffled in the fog.

Now to get back to where it was warm and dry. Quickly, thought Vinnie, for if they waited too long, Perry might send the steerage children directly down. If they could get to the passageway astern, they might avoid the press of people at the main entrance to the saloon.

24

"You take the girls," she said to Lottie. "Toby, you keep the other boys with you and follow Lottie." She stepped down with Joel in her arms and helped Grace slide to the deck. "This way," she directed.

Joel tried to struggle out of her grasp. "Let me say good-bye to Piggy."

She tightened her grip on him. "You can come back to visit the pig later," she promised. "When the sun comes out."

"Everyone is here," Grace protested. "I want to see them. The whole world is here."

"Hurry!" Vinnie gasped, for there seemed to be other people with the idea of getting away from the crowd. Feeling her way past a lifeboat and rounding the bulkhead, she flung herself at the doorway. The children complained of the darkness.

"Never mind. Hold on. Feel how warm it is."

Joel's arms tightened around her neck; she could scarcely breathe. The passage seemed to go on and on. Then voices broke through from behind. One of the boys cried out; a man's oath covered his cry.

"I have children here," Vinnie called back anxiously. "Do you want to pass us?"

"What are you doing here? This is the way to the crew's quarters."

"We didn't mean to. We thought we could get to the saloon."

"Hold on then, miss. We'll go ahead and show you the way."

As best she could, Vinnie hauled her troop to one side. Several men passed her. Up ahead there was a clanking and squeal and a sudden rectangle of dim light. "This way," called one of the men.

"Oh, thank you. Thank you."

All the children sprang toward the light. "Not like that," Vinnie cried out, as the ship lurched. "In line." She could feel a shudder underfoot, then a forward thrust. Her heart surged with relief. "There! The ship's started." The passengers on deck were

25

in an uproar that sounded like cheering. The ship shuddered again; it seemed to leap ahead. This was almost like the storm again, except that there was no wind, no crashing waves. The passengers outside were beside themselves.

"Better wait," one of the men called to her.

"Will you come back for us?" Vinnie asked him, but he was already gone, the others with him.

The ship staggered, hurling them to the floor. Then it righted itself.

"There," Vinnie said again. "Soon we'll be on our way."

"Why are you talking like that?" Lottie shouted. "There's something wrong." She charged back into the darkness.

"Don't you stir," Vinnie commanded the other children. "Those men know where we are. They'll be back."

Toby said, "Get them down."

"Down," she directed, her heart pounding. She drew Joel into her lap.

The ship became a wounded beast. It reared so steeply that even seated on the floor, the children went flying against the wall. Vinnie grabbed Grace and Nell. Joel rolled from her lap, but Toby caught him. The ship let out a grinding howl; the beast was being torn apart.

Outside, the commotion was different now. Vinnie could hear shouted orders: "Loose the boats!" and "Women and children!" and "Lines!"

"What is it?" Joel cried.

"A shipwreck," Toby told him.

"Is that it?" Joel looked out at her from under Toby's arms.

"They know we're here," she said. "And they're calling for women and children. We'll stay till they're ready for us, for we don't want you slipping under the rail."

Grace clutched at her. "What's going to happen?"

"We're about to put to sea in the boats. We'll be fine, because the sea is calm now. Another ship will come and save us."

26

"Maybe Mother's ship will come," said Grace.

Lottie crawled up to them, white-faced and panting, her voice softened by terror. "Water at that end. The door's shut, but the water's coming in anyway. I don't see how it can."

The ship heaved once more. A wave came slopping up from the darkness. One of the twins shrieked. "Hold hands," Vinnie shouted, tripping on the oversized cloak. She grabbed Joel and attached his hand to Grace's. "Everyone come!"

The door the men had gone through brought the children into another passageway. Vinnie could hear crashes and cries. Probably the crew was attending to the steerage passengers, getting them out of the rising water. It would make sense to bring them up ahead of Vinnie's little group. Yet it seemed so dangerous here. Where should they turn?

Toby wrenched aside a hatch cover nearly above them. There was the deck. Vinnie scrambled up first, then lay flat to haul out the others. The ship kept flinging them down. Where was the crew? She didn't dare look for help until all the children were clinging to one another and to a line that crossed the slanting deck. Only then did she pull herself to her feet. Voices drifted through the fog, yet she couldn't single out a figure or a face. Had they all gone forward?

Inching her way along, she came to huge iron rings where before she had leaned against one of the lifeboats. And over there was the pig crate, the pigs in a heap because of the pitch of the deck. One pig which lay on its side seemed to think it was running; its legs thrashed. The crate had slid to the rail; a single line kept it from crashing through into the water.

"Mr. Powdermaker!" she called. "Master Perry! Please, is someone here?"

No one answered from the foredeck. Shouts floated across the water.

"Get back. Row seaward."

"This way. Open water."

Vinnie crept toward the rail, hand over hand on the line. Now she could see three boats, a fourth just slipping out of sight. They were packed with people.

"Oh, please," she called. Linking her arm around the line, she cupped her hands to her mouth. "Please come back for us. We are children. Please."

The rowers in the nearest boat ceased rowing. Someone shouted, "Who are you?"

Another declared, "I thought everyone was accounted for."

"I have the Stott children and my cousin and six others."

Voices broke in, until one shouted the others down. "We can't possibly fit them in. We'd lose all in the attempt."

"Please," Vinnie pleaded. "We heard you calling for women and children, and I thought . . . we were told. . . ."

"Row on," ordered the voice of authority.

"Mr. Powdermaker!" Vinnie screamed as the boat moved away from the ship. "Help us!" She couldn't believe that they were leaving her clinging to the deck beside the pigs, with the other children waiting to be rescued. "Is there another boat?" she called. "Please, someone, tell me what to do."

"Lavinia!"

The call came out of the fog, across the water. Vinnie could see nothing. But she heard Mr. Powdermaker say, "I thought they were aft, with the first group." Another boat hove into view. It too was jammed with people huddled together, all but the tall figure of Mr. Powdermaker, who was directing the rowers toward the ship.

Vinnie waved, and a woman she didn't know, but whom she would always remember, waved in return and said, "There, child, we're coming."

"Grace? Joel?" That was Perry.

"Other side," Vinnie told him. "I'll get them."

Mr. Powdermaker was already issuing orders. A babbling broke

28

out in the boat. She couldn't hear him anymore. She met the little ones midway and brought them along to the crate. Grace screamed when she saw how close they were to the water. "Hush!" Lottie snapped as she set the twins in a niche between the crate and a coiled line. "How can we hear what we are to do next?" Grace was silenced, though her body shook with sobs. Toby handed Joel down beside her. The other boys, Jack and Willie, were the last across to the crate.

"All right," Mr. Powdermaker was saying to the people in the boat. "All right, you needn't come closer. I'll bring the children to us." Now he spoke to Vinnie. "That rope. Unfasten it. No, no!" he cried, as she reached for the knot that held the pig crate. "The other end." But as soon as she began to follow the line upward, Mr. Powdermaker screamed," No! Can't you hear me? The pigs first."

He must have lost his senses. What did he mean, pigs first? It was women and children first, for mercy's sake, not pigs.

"Listen," Perry shouted to her, "let the pigs out."

Vinnie and Toby struggled to open the crate. Everyone was yelling at once. When the door finally slid back, the pigs wouldn't budge. Mr. Powdermaker screamed at Vinnie to leave the pigs to Toby and get back to the knot.

She crawled along the slanting deck, the great cloak binding her skirt to her knees. Turning, she saw one of the pigs skitter sideways and disappear over the side. The next pig was squealing as it followed the first into the water. She tore at the knot that fastened the line to a ring, but it was too big and too tight. The ship shifted again. As it rolled, it sent out a wave that shot the crowded boat upward. When the wave pushed on, Mr. Powdermaker was no longer standing. He was no longer in the boat.

The rowers pulled away from the sinking ship. "Wait," cried Perry, others joining him. The woman who had waved was one of these. Standing now herself, she called for rescue rather than

29

cowardly retreat. Meanwhile, Mr. Powdermaker, gasping and spluttering, scrambled onto the partly submerged deck and went right to work on the knot.

"Sir," said Toby, "I can't get the last pig out. It's dead."

"Leave it," Mr. Powdermaker told him. He turned, the freed line in his hand. "All children on top of the crate. Hurry. Hold on to the slats. That's right, facedown, all of you." The crate was afloat. "You too," he said to Vinnie. "Whatever happens, stay with them. If we can't reach the boat this way, use this pole to keep clear of the ship." He was shoving a boat hook into her hands. "Hurry!"

But she couldn't hurry with the cloak dragging her and the crate floating off. She found herself face to face with the pig. It seemed to be eyeing her through the slats, floating too, its mouth agape. She felt Mr. Powdermaker pushing her up with the others. There was Toby, hauling her, while his legs acted like extra arms, pinning down Nell and Joel. The boat hook drifted off, only to be grabbed by Mr. Powdermaker and returned to her. "You'll need this to push away debris too," he said, spitting water. She nodded, her eyes stinging. "Balance," he commanded. "Now, I'm going back to stand up so I can throw the line to the lifeboat." He vanished for an instant. Then she saw him on what remained of the wheelhouse roof. He hurled a coiled line, but it fell short. He gathered it to him.

The woman who had waved called out to him. As the line whirred over Vinnie's head, the woman and Perry stretched way out over the water to catch it. There was a report like a thunder-clap. Mr. Powdermaker came hurtling after the line, a coil still in his hand. Even before he hit the water, the shock wave from the ship sprang up. It left behind the crate with all the children, but it hit the lifeboat broadside, slapped it down, and dumped its passengers into the sea.

Vinnie could see people swimming toward the boat. Others

were clinging to it already, while some, screaming and flailing, went under. She couldn't see Mr. Powdermaker at all.

Someone reached out toward the crate. Vinnie strained to take the hand, but just as she clasped the slippery fingers, Nell and Joel began to slide off. Balance, she thought, retreating, or she would lose the children. Yet a moment later when she saw something else bobbing close by, she tried again to catch it. This time Lottie and Toby leaned the other way. She groped in the water, only to find she had the dead pig. She let go with a cry.

Now she could see one or two people supported by floating timbers. Where was the boat? Were they drifting apart? She caught a glimpse of an oar floating toward her. No, not floating; there was someone pushing it. Master Perry! As the oar nudged up beside her, he tried to scramble onto the crate, which instantly dipped. The children screamed. He was too big, too heavy. Couldn't he see that?

Water gushed from his nose and mouth. Maybe he couldn't hear the children's cries. One of the boys lost hold. It seemed as though nothing mattered to Master Perry but gaining the pig crate.

Toby extended his legs over the water where the boy was thrashing wildly and gulping seawater. "Willie," shouted Toby, "grab hold on me." But Willie couldn't help himself. Toby had to go after him and drag him to the crate. Vinnie helped haul him up. Toby was just hitching himself up as well when Perry elbowed and squirmed so hard that the crate started to sink again. This time Toby was tossed off.

"Willie won't hold on," wailed Grace.

Perry kicked the water, trying to get his legs up.

"Children," Vinnie gasped, "women and children." She shimmied back to offset Perry's weight and thrust the boat hook out toward Toby.

"Grace," Perry yelled, "push the dead boy off."

31

"He's not dead," cried Lottie.

Vinnie told her to make room for Toby. They would rebalance themselves so that Perry could hold on without pulling anyone else down. But first Vinnie had to reach Toby with that pole. It kept falling short. It was so hard to aim it without striking the water and losing it. She swung it wide, too wide. It swatted Perry a glancing blow that knocked him back. His reddened eyes stared at her in disbelief, then closed as if in sleep.

Horrified, Vinnie watched his body straighten in the water until he seemed to be standing upright. Only there was nothing for him to stand on. With a glance that showed her Toby gripping the far side of the crate, Vinnie drew a breath and dropped over the side. To catch Perry's sleeve, she had only to put out the hand she had refused him before.

They had to tip the crate to roll Perry on. Then they settled the children so that the crate was fairly balanced. It was all they could do. Vinnie and Toby had to hang on at the edge, for there was no way they could climb out of the water now.

The water was cold, but not numbing. It just felt tighter and tighter. Vinnie linked her arms with Toby's and with the slats. She tried to kick aside debris with her feet. There was a body floating face down; woman's clothing fanned out, giving it a bloated look. Vinnie turned her face from it and found herself staring into the shiny dark eyes of a rat clinging to the back of a chair that bobbed in the water. The rat was motionless. Vinnie saw herself like that—staring, helpless. All were equal in this sea, all in the same race to outlast the ones who floated on their faces. Who would read the prayer for the dead over that woman? "I am the resurrection and the life, saith the Lord," Vinnie recited silently.

Above her head, Grace whimpered and Joel complained of being crowded. " 'He that believeth in me,' " Vinnie whispered, " 'though he were dead, yet shall he live. . . .' "

Toby, with eyes closed, said, "Willie may be all right." So she didn't finish the prayer.

She was getting drowsy. All that seemed to matter was letting her head fall sideways, cushioned on her arm.

From far off she heard a cry. Someone over her, someone with the look of screaming. She knew she was about to wake up. Let it be home, Vinnie thought. Let it be Mama calling me. I won't mind, even if it's to send me off to the matchbox factory or out to the fields.

"Vinnie!" Someone had her by the hair. She turned as far as she could, twisting her body. Only there was no body. Feeling nothing, she opened her eyes. There was the contorted face of her cousin.

"Why, Charlotte," she murmured. "Lottie. Whatever is the matter?" To her astonishment, Lottie rose up. Then she wasn't Lottie anymore. She was a sack of turnips, all floppy with lumps, flung across a man's shoulder.

Vinnie was drawn up too. "No," she cried, trying to free herself, "we'll sink. Too heavy. Children. No." But whoever it was lifting her turned out to be much stronger than she. He had her like another sack. Then she was set down among the children.

All about them, figures moved in and out of the gray fog, over black rocks, through water the color of dull pewter, among slimy fronds tinged reddish brown. Still everything seemed gray to her; she might have been looking through glass covered with webs and soot.

"Grace?" she murmured. "Joel?"

Lottie emerged through the film of gray, her face hovering over Vinnie's for a moment. Vinnie thought she caught sight of her again on the back of one of the silent gray men who swarmed all around these rocks. For a little while Vinnie kept track of her cousin's progress up the sheer rock face. Straight up into swirling

33

mists went Lottie—if it was Lottie—on the back of one of those silent creatures.

Then Vinnie found herself gazing at a smaller child, whose arms were firmly attached around the neck of its bearer. Who was the child? Vinnie couldn't tell. She felt someone take her by the shoulders. A rope tightened around her. She managed to whisper, "Women and children first." She thought she was in the water again and began to struggle. Then she was dangling, aloft. Beside her a gray man leaned away from the rock and guided her as she was drawn slowly upward. Once he was forced to let her go. She twirled, now facing cliff, now empty grayness, and now catching a glimpse of him swinging away and back until his toes caught rock and his hand steadied her once more.

She was not afraid, but her hands and feet ached, the life squeezed out of them. Every gulp of air tore at her throat. Tears stung her eyes.

Everything was magnified, toes and hands, a face, the edge of a cliff with something green, enormous spears of green that folded between her fingers. She was lying facedown, and her fingers clutched the green spears and ripped them, while her body heaved and heaved.

Darkness deeper than the ocean dragged her down. "He that believeth," she began to pray inside her head. "Believeth." But the silent prayer foundered. Enough, she thought. Enough.

four

Once upon a time . . . Vinnie didn't know the voice, but she recognized the lilt of the storyteller. *Once upon a time there was a little match girl. . . .* Oh, thought Vinnie, *that* story. *Once upon a time there was a little match girl and her mama. . . .* Vinnie smiled.

The matchbox factory is a shed behind the cobbler's house. Vinnie works beside her mother while Lottie plays in the yard with the younger children. There is a drain that becomes a little river when it rains. The small children sail boats made of broken boxes. Lottie comes begging for more. "Vinnie won't give me her bits of wood," Lottie complains. "Give them to her," Mama orders, reaching over and pulling this one and that from Vinnie's little pile. Then Mama coughs and coughs, so there can be no argument. Vinnie must hurry now, because she is behind. If she fails to make enough boxes, she will lose her work at the table to another.

Later, at Auntie's, Lottie cries because of her chilblains. That makes Uncle cross. Mama clutches herself between bouts of coughing; lessons begin.

"What is the world?" asks Mama.

"The earth we dwell on," the children reply together.

35

"Who made it?"

Again they recite as one, "The great and good God."

Auntie says, "Leave off with Lottie. Let her sleep, and she'll forget the hurting fingers. If you ask me, Vinnie would be better off with her supper and sleep too. She won't grow on education."

"Yes, she will," Mama retorts. "The day will come. She'll stand apart."

"What good has learning ever done you?"

Without replying, Mama turns back to her daughter. "Who made it?" she demands.

Vinnie has already answered that question, but she is afraid to say so. "The great and good God?" she asks in a small voice.

"Speak out! With firmness."

Uncle is pacing; he is ready to fly into a rage. Vinnie shivers.

Auntie tells Mama, "You asked that one before."

Mama stoutly continues. "Are there not many things in it you would like to know about?"

Vinnie nudges Lottie. "Yes, very much," they reply with all the eagerness they can muster. Now comes the lesson. Tonight it is geography.

"America," says Mama with venom on her tongue, "is a land that is mostly wilderness. Even the cities. And the people are without manners. The capital city of Massachusetts is Boston and the capital of the entire country is Washington, and that is also the name of the first president, Washington. Americans have no king or queen, which is why they resemble wayward children who want the discipline of a loving parent. God save the Queen."

"God save the Queen," Vinnie repeats, as she does each night at the close of her lesson. Only now may she go to the soup pan. There is a parsnip in her portion. She takes it in her fingers, but Mama slaps her hand. The parsnip drops to the floor and is snatched away by the cat.

Vinnie sips slowly. It is important to make the supper last.

36

That way you can fool your stomach into thinking you have put a great deal into it.

Mama tells Vinnie to mind her manners. "One day you may work in a shop or go into service like me and work in a fine house where you can better yourself."

In bed with Lottie, there is story time. Vinnie savors her mama's words and learns them by heart. "Once upon a time there was a little match girl. . . ." The little girl strikes one match after another to keep warm. She thinks she sees rooms with fires burning and tables laid with food for her. Then, just as the spark of life dims, she is found to be a princess who was banished by an evil ruler. There is proof, a crown that fits no head but hers. Mama's fingers encircle Vinnie's head. "Like that," she says. And the little match girl lives happily ever after.

This story takes root inside Vinnie. Like her own limbs, it supports her as she grows. Yet a day comes when she is much older, when she is with the Stott family and reading aloud to Joel and Grace, when she reaches the end of this story and is horrified to find that the little match girl has frozen to death. Vinnie shows the heartless print to Mrs. Stott, only to be assured it is quite correct. How can it be? Vinnie must defend Mama's ending, the princess and the crown.

Vinnie didn't want that story now. It might end wrong. It all depended on the storyteller, and Vinnie didn't know who that was. So she asked for another story instead, and the voice began again: *Once upon a time there was a girl on a big ship. . . .*

So this story must be about Grace, thought Vinnie, or else about Nell and the twins. Only, what twins? Vinnie wondered. Who was Nell?

Her father was a sailor, chanted the storyteller. *He sailed upon the sea. . . .*

No, Vinnie objected. Grace's father is not a sailor. Mr. Stott is an engineer. He makes bridges.

37

Her father was a sailor, the voice went on.

If it's only a story, thought Vinnie, maybe it doesn't have to be true.

Auntie objects to Mama filling the children's heads with fancies. "I thought you gave up fairy tales," grumbles Auntie, "when your prince was lost and the wicked king sent—"

"That will do!" cries Vinnie's mama. "You promised never to mention—"

"What wicked king?" Vinnie sits up. "Is there a true lost prince?"

"Auntie didn't mean it," snaps Mama, but she casts a secret look at Auntie.

Vinnie longs to ask more. Maybe some day when Mama is feeling happy and well she will tell her secret to Vinnie. But the moments never seem right; the happy times turn thin and brittle. Then Mama's voice grows so weak that the lessons and stories cease, and Vinnie knows there is no use waiting anymore.

The field gang sets off in the early morning darkness that feels like night. It's miles to the fields, and miles to trudge back home, again in the dark.

One night Vinnie comes home through wind and rain into absolute stillness. Auntie strips the sodden skirt and blouse from her and wraps her in Mama's shawl. Mama's shawl that has served as a blanket these last weeks. And never a word is spoken then, nor when Vinnie has her stiff porridge. Vinnie has to chew hard to get the pasty lumps down. Auntie clasps and unclasps her hands watching Vinnie struggle with her supper.

Suddenly, in the darkness, Lottie sits up in bed. "Vinnie?" She looks across the room at Auntie and Vinnie. "Your mama's in heaven," Lottie declares.

Auntie takes the bowl from Vinnie's shaking hands and leads her to the bed.

"Your hair's wet," Lottie tells her. "It's cold."

Vinnie can't stop shivering. There is a lump of porridge glued to the roof of her mouth.

Once upon a time there was a little match girl who set out to find a secret. Vinnie crawls along the row of turnips, clawing up the cold roots and shaking the soil from them.

"Vinnie, hey, you're slowing down!" calls Betsy Rood across the furrow. "He's seen you. He's coming after."

Vinnie whacks off the dirt, flings the turnip into her sack, and digs out the next one. For a while she keeps up with Betsy and the others.

Before long, though, she is telling her story again. She finds a rhythm with the turnip pulling that matches the words in her head. The day drags on. The rows of turnips seem to stretch all the way from Zanzibar to Mississippi. Those places roll down her tongue, the names her mama made her learn so that someday she might stand apart. "Zanzibar," she murmurs, "Niagara, Alexandria." She doesn't know where most of those places are. They are just notes from a forgotten song playing their secret music in her head. Lurching with the rhythm of it, she is parted from the sack tied to her shoulder. The turnips tumble out.

Stopping, she sees the little boy marching gamely, heedlessly, along the wall. He'll fall, she thinks, oh, he'll fall. She staggers to her feet. The sack and turnips are left behind. Later, when she is wrapped in pain and confusion, the overseer grumbles about the mess of turnips sprawled in the field. He complains until he is given a little money for his trouble. She can't know then that she will never see him again.

Nor can she know that the race to reach the little boy on the wall will lead her to America. It isn't till more than a year later, after the magic lantern show for Grace's birthday, that she learns this. The magic lantern pictures American scenes of forests and soaring trees. Mrs. Stott says that in North American people tap the maples when the sap runs and make sugar from it. Joel and

Grace can taste it in the birthday sweets. Vinnie's heart beats wildly at the sight of those trees. She doesn't know why.

The magic lantern also shows pictures of Indians and waterfalls and the Capitol building in Washington, which Vinnie recalls from her lessons is spelled with an *o*, and New York and Boston, capital of Massachusetts (*capital* spelled with an *a*), and Springfield, Illinois. Vinnie is so caught up in these scenes, Mrs. Stott's voice fades. Vinnie hears rushing water and the wind moaning high in the tops of trees with snow heavy on their branches.

When the lights go on, everyone is talking at once, for Mr. and Mrs. Stott have just announced that before long the children may actually see some of those places. Mr. Stott must return to Canada, where Mrs. Stott and the children will join him in a few months time. First Mrs. Stott must arrange for the homeless children she intends to bring across the Atlantic.

She has already written to Mr. Powdermaker, who is in shipping and who advises her. Mr. Powdermaker himself has sent homeless children out to Ohio with fair success. There are so many things to be seen to before the family will be ready to join Mr. Stott.

Joel catches sight of Vinnie at the back of the room. "Will Vinnie come too?" he wants to know.

"Of course," Mr. Stott assures him, but Vinnie shakes her head.

That evening, after Grace and Joel are put to bed, Mrs. Stott calls Vinnie into the drawing room. "You may have a sweet," Mrs. Stott tells her.

Vinnie takes a maple sweet from the little dish on the table. She holds it between her fingers. If she presses too hard, it will turn to paste.

"Mr. Stott and I would be grieved if you did not come. We think of you as part of our family now."

"My aunt . . ." Vinnie begins. She doesn't know how to tell Mrs. Stott that her mama loathed America.

40

"You feel obliged to stay because of your aunt?"

"She took care of my mama," blurts Vinnie. "And now she's hard pressed. She'd go into service, but Lottie is a care. I promised Mama to help."

Mrs. Stott nods thoughtfully. She'll see what can be done. Vinnie can't imagine what she means, but she is distracted now by the maple sweet, which has begun to ooze. She raises the sugary mess to keep it from soiling her apron.

"You'd best pop it in your mouth," Mrs. Stott advises, rising from her chair and going to stand at the window.

Vinnie does so, grateful that Mrs. Stott has turned her back. But Vinnie can't swallow. She holds the sticky sweet on her tongue, her senses reeling with the heat of it in her mouth. She grips the back of a chair. It is only a sweet, she tells herself, I am not used to such things. She swallows and swallows. Even after it goes down, its essence remains, heady and sharp and clotted with disturbing images.

Glancing in the mirror, she sees herself, her dark hair drawn back, the heat on her cheeks, a spot of maple sugar at the corner of her mouth. There is a strand of hair come free. Swiftly she tucks it back, but it sticks to her sugary fingers and falls over her eyes. Through the dark strands, she sees not her own face, but another surrounded by steam rising sweetly from a bubbling cauldron. She strains toward the mirror, toward the face, but it is gone, like someone in a throng—someone you happen to notice and think you must know. Once gone, though, you cannot even recall the features that struck you so.

Vinnie's eyes were open. She stared into a face. She tried to speak, but she only made a sound like a baby crow squawking in its nest. The face vanished.

Was that the storyteller? If only she could call it back and ask for another story. She would like one out of her book of Greek heroes. How about the tale of Orpheus, the prince of minstrels whose song cast a spell of longing on a grounded ship? *My father*

41

was a sailor, he sailed upon the sea. Then Orpheus began his magic song, and the good ship *Argo* heard him and rushed into the whispering sea. Phrases from the book came torn and ragged. *Once upon a time the heroes rowed away. . . .*

Then Vinnie yielded to waking. She let this story carry her out of the darkness. *And they ran the ship ashore, but they had no strength left. . . . And they crawled out on the pebbles, and sat down and wept.* Vinnie listened intently, drifting toward the light. *For the houses and the trees were all altered; and all the faces which they saw were strange. And the people crowded round and asked them, "Who are you that you sit weeping here?" "We are the sons of your princes, who sailed out many a year ago. . . ."*

Someone held a cup to Vinnie's lips. The face was there again in the dimness. It didn't matter who it was. Vinnie understood now that she herself was the storyteller she'd been listening to. *My father was a sailor, a prince,* she began. *I sailed upon the sea, upon the good ship* Roger F. Laing. *And the heroes rowed away. And all the faces were strange.*

This time the face remained.

"Thank you," Vinnie murmured.

The woman stared at her with very blue eyes.

Vinnie sipped again. How hard it was to swallow. She could hear a little whine like a puppy or a kitten. She tried to call. "Lottie?" She waited, holding her breath, and all was silent. Even the whining had stopped. But when she drew a breath to call again, the sound came back. "Joel! Grace!" She gasped for air. More whining. Something on her chest was squeezing the breath out of her.

She tried taking the air in tiny sips as she had done with the broth. The whine came in jagged sighs. She wanted to tell the woman she wasn't crying, but the woman was gone.

Vinnie propped herself up on her hand. A dark place. Very warm, and full of unfamiliar smells. Where were the children? The bedding rustled as she sank back; rough homespun protected

42

her from stalky bristles. She could hear flames spurting up, a comforting sound that nearly blotted out the sharp, ugly wheeze that came from her throat.

When she looked for the fireplace, she saw the woman stirring the fire. Vinnie tried to speak to her. "The children?" It came out a croaked whisper.

After the woman finished settling the turf on the fire, Vinnie heard her speak for the first time. The words were like the fluttering of summer moths around a lamp, soft and rapid and in a strange language.

"Oh, please." Vinnie propped herself again. She sat up. She was in a raised cupboard in a wall, surrounded by stone. "I'm in charge of those other children." She let her feet down to the earthen floor. "Where are they?" With her hands, she outlined the shape of Grace as though the child stood before her. She brought her arms up so that they seemed to be holding Joel. "The little ones," she pleaded hoarsely.

The woman shook her head, her long black braids swinging. She dipped a cup in a pot.

Vinnie rocked an imaginary infant. "Please," she rasped.

The woman set down the cup and took Vinnie in her arms. She held her, rocked her, and crooned in those fluttery syllables—the notes full of air and sadness.

five 🏵

Time passed in a kind of twilight. At first Vinnie slept and woke without any sense of the hours or days. Often her waking was so dreamlike and dim that it seemed no more than the farthest edges of sleep.

The woman moved in silence through that twilight. Sometimes she tended the fire or sat on the floor turning a grinding stone to make meal. Sometimes she stood by the door pulling a thread of yarn from a cloud of wool that dropped twirling on a spindle. Occasionally the woman went away. Gradually Vinnie came to realize that the absences happened regularly. For Vinnie, this was the first reckoning of order.

She began to see and feel beyond the closeness of the bed cupboard and the dark room with its single door. The cottage had no windows, but there was an opening in the roof thatch over the central fireplace. Bird carcasses strung on a line beneath the opening had a restless look about them whenever the wind blew hard. Vinnie watched them starting turns they never finished. Weird shadows danced on the bare earthen floor.

When she was strong enough, Vinnie made her way to the door. A short wall spanned the opening in front of her, a baffle against the wind. Beyond it Vinnie could see rocks and turf, but little else, for fog clung to the land.

Whenever the woman left the cottage, Vinnie went to the door, straining to catch the sound of voices. She imagined Joel's laughter or Grace's call, but these were only the cries of seafowl over distant waves.

She always scooted back to bed before the woman returned. She didn't know why. The woman would help her come to the fire in the middle of the room; the door was never closed. Yet Vinnie felt she had to conceal her habit of standing at the door, listening.

Without a word spoken, a kind of language was born between them. Yielding to the woman's simple routine, Vinnie sensed that she was healing and that the woman knew the healing had to take its course.

When Vinnie attempted to bathe herself and wash her clothes, the woman stood back with absorbed interest. Vinnie soon used up all the water she had heated over the fire. Clutching a blanket around her, she tried to dip some more from the stone basin. Quickly the woman rose; gently she pulled Vinnie aside and completed the task for her. Vinnie wondered whether the children were being kept as she was. Who would wash them and attend to their soiled clothes?

When she put on her clean things, she felt new and more vital somehow. And closer to the end of this waiting.

One day it rained so hard the woman didn't go out at her customary time. She paced the small room and came as close to fidgeting as Vinnie had ever seen her.

The woman's restlessness was contagious. Vinnie sat in the bed cupboard, her legs dangling, kicking the stone wall with her heels. Suddenly, in a rush of heat and yearning, she clutched herself. Oh, speak to me, she pleaded without uttering a sound. Please, let us talk. Teach me your language. I'm clever; I'm a good reader, though not so good at sums. I know prayers and songs and history and geography and rhymes. . . . She clutched herself until she ached.

After a while the woman took up her spindle and began to pull and twist the thread of wool. The wind howled like a flayed beast. Vinnie sank back into her cupboard darkness. For the first time sleep did not come.

The next day they were without milk. Vinnie was astonished that it had taken this long for her to realize the nature of the woman's daily outings. But she must have been worried about the cow, because even though it was still raining hard, she threw on an extra shawl and set out. Vinnie watched the rain pelting the gray stone. Something out there moved. Vinnie stared. A person? Was it Master Perry?

It wasn't. This boy was shorter. His lumpy rain-soaked jacket seemed too big for him. He cast a sidelong glance uphill. Was he afraid? For an instant their eyes met. Yet he came no closer. Once, slowly, he wiped his hand across his face, mopping away the rain and pushing his red hair off his forehead. The next moment he was just as wet as before.

Suddenly he wheeled and ducked down behind the wind wall. Vinnie moved to the doorway. Why couldn't she see him? The rain seemed to be rinsing away the fog. Gazing out and down the steep, rocky slope, she caught another glimpse of him. He was bounding like a goat from rock to rock, a black-and-white dog running circles around him. He never once looked back, but kept on, his course jagged with turns and backtracks, until suddenly the earth swallowed him. Or so it seemed.

When the woman returned, Vinnie was back at the fire. As usual they exchanged no greeting. The woman set down her jug, dropped her outer shawl at the door and stepped over it. Walking to the hearth, she stooped toward the fire.

Vinnie rose. She took the under shawl from the woman's shoulders. It was heavy with rain. She spread it wide and went to pick up the outer shawl, which lay in a heap, the water running in a muddy rivulet toward the hearth. She picked up the jug of milk too and began to skim bits of wool and dirt specks from it. Dipping out a small amount, she mixed into it a few handfuls of meal. This she stirred and set at the edge of the fire, just as she had seen the woman do. Then Vinnie fetched her own cloak and drew it over the woman's back. She handed her a cup full of warm milk and meal, reversing days—or was it weeks?—of this simple gesture.

Vinnie saw the woman to the bed cupboard, where she lay huddled and shivering under a blanket. What else could Vinnie do for her? She eyed the bird carcasses hanging from the thatch. She recalled watching the woman slit a dried bird and cook it in a pot with greens she must have gathered on her outings. Gingerly Vinnie dragged the stool, climbed on it, and reached for one of the birds. It was stiff, hard as bark. Broth, thought Vinnie, as the woman's teeth began to chatter. Sometimes when Auntie could afford an old fowl, she would leave it simmering all day until the scanty meat fell from the bones. Add an onion, Vinnie thought, searching every recess and finding no vegetables of any kind.

Mrs. Stott's cook made splendid soups with mutton and barley and turnips and carrots. Vinnie's mouth watered. Suddenly a true, ravenous hunger seized her. Surely there must be something else to boil with one small dry bird. The rain had subsided to a drizzle, so she took Mrs. Stott's cloak and set out in search of greens. She found a steep path winding uphill through coarse, soaked grass, but she saw no greens to pick. Soon her legs were trembling. She had to clutch the spongy ground for support. Then she seized a fistful of nettles. The sting was so sharp and sudden she cried out. Dropping to her knees, she rubbed her palms on cool, wet grass.

Out of the corner of her eye, she saw something dart away. There was a blat of a sheep, then an answering blat from somewhere. If she kept on, she might find the cow and the cow shed, maybe other people. Maybe the children. Where were the men who carried them up the cliff? They couldn't be far.

She continued on until there, ahead of her, was a small round turf-roofed stone hut; beyond it, another, its grassy domed roof like a head of thick green hair. Scrambling up to the nearest hut, she peered inside and saw stacks of birds. Disappointed, she retreated. Maybe she should go back before she was too worn out. She might wrap her hand in the cloak and pick nettles for the broth.

Turning, she saw the ocean far below. It tumbled and heaved, a mountain of churning slag. Were those black specks way down there the rocks where she and the others had landed from the pig crate? Those rocks looked jagged and treacherous. How could anyone tossed on them survive?

It was dizzying to look down like that. She couldn't help rocking back, her hand flung out for balance. Another hand gripped it. Vinnie gasped. Standing beside her was the red-haired boy. The black-and-white dog held back a little, watching them.

He said, "Don't be afraid."

He spoke English! But he was dressed like no English boy she had ever seen—a thick, loose shirt under his waistcoat and baggy trousers. His feet were bare.

"Have you seen the others? My children?"

"There are new children in the village. And the big boy."

"Perry."

"He hasn't told me his name."

"Are they all right?"

"The island people are very good to children. They love them."

"Can you take me to them?"

He shook his head. "I'm not supposed to be here. I tried to speak with the big boy, but he wouldn't. Wouldn't hear me. I couldn't stay."

Thinking that was just like Perry to refuse to talk, she asked the boy his name.

"Andrew. Andrew Crabtree."

She smiled at him. It was good to speak again, to be understood. "I'm Lavinia Grey. Vinnie. Will you come back? Will you come every day?"

Andrew's face clouded. "I only came to warn you. . . ." He glanced toward the path. "You must hide your clothes. Keep them safe for later. One thing at a time, or else the villagers will search. And what they search for they find."

Vinnie couldn't understand. "You mean they'll steal our clothes?"

"I haven't time to explain everything now. You should begin at once. Give me your cloak."

Vinnie clutched it to her.

"Give it to me. Trust me."

Slowly, with misgivings, Vinnie drew off Mrs. Stott's cloak and handed it to him. He nodded, then gestured at her skirt and blouse. "Next time I'll take one of those. Now go back before she comes."

"She won't. She caught a chill."

"Good," he said.

Good? Vinnie was shocked. Good that the woman who had nursed and cared for her lay shivering and miserable in a dreary little cottage all alone? She felt like snatching back her cloak. But he was ahead of her already, leading the way at a nimble trot that left her breathless again and weak.

He stopped beside a massive boulder. Shifting a flat stone, he showed Vinnie another beneath it. "Lay your clothing here," he directed, "and I'll gather it when I can. I have to leave you now."

"Why must you?"

"The tide," he said, bunching the cloak under his arm. "And don't say a word of me to her."

Her. The woman. "What's her name?"

"Peg," he told Vinnie. "Only you must pretend not to know."

Sullenly she met his eyes. Why should she believe him?

But he didn't wait for a promise. She watched as he pelted down toward the rocks below, the dog bounding past, until she lost sight of them both along the rough cliff. Of them and of her cloak.

By the third day of Peg's illness, the bird and nettle broth was gone. There remained only bird bones and bits of nettles turned to slime. After one bite, Peg touched her throat, shook her head, and pointed at Vinnie. To please her, Vinnie ate the next spoonful; the oily pulp tasted of fish. It was time to find some more greens.

Vinnie took the basket she had seen Peg use for carrying turfs. Peg hoisted it on her back, but Vinnie just slung it over her arm. When she reached the two round huts, she stood for a while to catch her breath. With the sun filtering through the clouds, the sea was shiny and as black as coal. It even rumbled like coal being dumped into a bin. Spray shot up against a solitary pillar of rock that reared up from the sea. Beyond it loomed a small, desolate island with a few sheep at the edge of its high cliff. They were somehow reassuring, fellow creatures after all. Only how on earth did they get there?

All at once she knew she had to end her isolation. She would look for the children, the village. She would get help for Peg too.

She turned her back to the sea and set out. For a while the landscape didn't change. She climbed to a ridge where she found a beaten track. Hoping it led to a cow shed, she followed along it, but all she passed were more domed huts. She didn't even stop to look inside them. She was tempted to climb still higher for a wider view, but she was afraid of losing her way back to Peg. Besides, higher up, the bitter wind was flaying. How could she have been so stupid as to give her cloak to Andrew? Perhaps he would never show up again now that he had it. Angry at herself, she trudged on.

Suddenly the land fell away. The track descended, winding to soften the steep drop. Far ahead, it leveled out again, tiny now.

She caught her breath. There was the village, a single row of cottages like Peg's, all of them facing a wall that was their only protection from the wind that swept up from the bay below them. The slopes above the cottages were dotted with little huts and tiny walled fields. And farther along, past the row of cottages, the track skirted two larger buildings before it wound on down to the crescent beach.

"Ssstop!"

Vinnie whipped around as Andrew appeared from behind a boulder. "I'm looking for my children. I'm getting help for Peg. She's worse."

"The villagers can't do anything for her. They all have it. They call it the boat cold. It happens every time a boat comes."

"They get it from a *boat?*"

"From people. From you and others."

Then who was taking care of the children? No doubt the adults who had also been saved. "What did you do with my cloak?" she demanded.

"Hid it. I told you. I looked under the rock for your dress," he added accusingly. "I expected to find you in homespun by now. It's not easy for me to come and fetch things."

What did he mean? He didn't sound like a simpleton; still, there must be something awry with his wits. Vinnie faced him. "You'll not get anything more from me. But if you tell me what you're about, I won't give you away."

He seemed to be weighing her resistance. He nodded. His eyes never ceased roaming the hill.

She leaned against the sun-warm rock. "I'm cold without my cloak."

"They'll give you a warm shawl. There's nothing they won't do for you. For any of you."

"Then what are you afraid of?"

"Them."

He was speaking riddles, and she was beginning to feel irritated.

51

Soon she would have to return to Peg; she hadn't even picked the greens. "Is there bread in the village?"

"Bannocks, if anyone's recovered enough to have baked. When I came here, they rescued more than thirty people from our ship. This time of year too, winter coming on. The islanders fed us all the food they had put by for themselves till spring. By the time a ship was able to stop here and take the shipwrecked people away, the islanders were too weak to carry on with their spring work. They'd deprived themselves to feed the people."

"Surely the rescued people sent back food afterward."

"Money. That's what they sent. The islanders didn't know what to do with it. The tacksman came next. He brought meal and tea and seed and salt. But for some of the old and the very young, it was too late; they were dead within the year. There aren't many children here. That's why the islanders like them so much. They want them."

The dog raised its head, then stood. Andrew grew still. A few sheep came into view, stopped at the sight of Andrew and Vinnie, then wheeled off. The dog lay down again.

"I don't see how anyone can starve," Vinnie remarked, "with all those sheep to eat."

"Many sheep were killed that winter. And all the cows."

She was about to assert that there must be at least one cow left, but thought better of giving away what might be Peg's secret. Instead she asked Andrew about himself. When had he come? Why was he still here? Where was he going?

"America," he said. "To my uncle in a city called Buffalo. What about you?"

"To Halifax. That's in Canada."

"I know that. I studied all about North America before they sent me out. And practiced the American way of speaking."

Vinnie couldn't help saying, "Well, you don't sound anything like Mr. Powdermaker, and he's American."

Andrew wasn't fazed. "It's a big country. I expect he's from a

52

different part, that's all. Like my mother, who speaks fine English, but with a touch of Scottish."

Vinnie said, "Anyway, I must go to the children now."

"But I haven't finished saying."

"It's getting late. I want to see them. I'm nurse to two of them, and another is my cousin."

"You don't look old enough for a nursemaid."

"Mrs. Stott took me in to train me. First I earned only my keep. That's the way it will work for the steerage children when they reach Canada. The little ones are to be adopted; the older ones go to families to work for a certain time."

Andrew looked mystified. "You're nurse to all those children?"

"No, I told you," Vinnie retorted, stepping back to the path. "Just to Grace and Joel Stott. They're to join their mother and father in Canada. I can't explain it all now."

Andrew ducked his head. "It's hard to stop talking after nearly two years without English. Except," he added, his hand on the dog's head, "to Kep here, but he doesn't talk back. It does feel good."

"You've been here nearly two years?" Now she was sure he was touched in the head. Who would stay on a desolate island instead of continuing on to Buffalo in America? If there was such a place. Most educated people, even nursemaids, knew that buffalo were some sort of wild cows. "Why didn't you go when everyone else was rescued?"

"The fishing boat couldn't take us all. And the next boat— Well, I expected to be taken on with others, but at the last minute one of the islanders spoke to the boatman. It's a kind of Gaelic. See, I know a bit of Gaelic because my granddad speaks it. Only island speech isn't exactly that. I understood some of it, though, about home and where I belonged. I supposed it had something to do with me being too late. That my family thought I was lost at sea and had sent one of my brothers on in my place. I thought I was to return home. On a different boat. Home."

"And that wasn't so?"

"I never found out. I was wearing the island clothes and learning island ways. It just went on that way. They taught me fowling on the crags to get the birds. They taught me about sheep and weaving. All the things island men do. All the things they need boys for. You see, they have only two of their own near grown like me. I was willing to earn my keep as long as I had to stay. And all that summer, no ship dared come inside the bay. Every day was fog." Andrew stopped. "I'll come no closer to the village. I'll leave you now."

Vinnie shook her head. "I still don't understand."

"Nor did I. Not until after the harvest was in, all the feathers baled and stored, the birds salted and dried, and the oil from them collected. It was only then, coming back to the village for the winter, that I saw the children. Three of them. Three children from our ship."

Vinnie searched in her mind for some explanation. She couldn't find any. She waited for Andrew to go on.

"Then over last winter," he told her, "I had time to think. And see. Two babies were born before spring. Neither lived. But the little boat orphans thrived. Everyone loved them."

Now Vinnie said, "Probably those three and you would have gone on the next boat, only there wasn't one."

"There wasn't one that first summer."

"And later?"

"Several, including the tacksman's boat to bring goods and take away the feathers and oil and tweed. There was even a boat of tourists, only the wind came up and they couldn't land. They looked at us through spyglasses."

"Why didn't you leave with the other ones?"

"Each time a boat landed, I was away. Once for the wool and once for the lambs and once on the far island, fowling. I had no way of getting back from there without an island rowing boat. Where they have me staying now, on the small near island, I can just get across to here at low tide. But there's no way off the far island, no way at all."

"And you think," Vinnie pronounced slowly, "that you were away each time because the islanders didn't want to lose you?"

"What else can I think?"

"Where were you when the tour boat came?"

"In the village."

"There! You see? You're imagining a plot to keep you here."

"I'm not imagining about the three children who are still here."

That stopped Vinnie for a moment. Then she declared stoutly, "Well, it won't happen that way again. Not with us here, not with the adults from the *Roger F. Laing*. They won't let it."

Andrew laughed quietly, without mirth. "There are no adults."

The sun was getting low. She had to shield her eyes against the glare. "Of course there are," she insisted. "I saw some."

"Where?" he challenged.

"In the water. Quite near me."

"There are no adults," he said again. "Not this time. I suppose the islanders learned from before. Last time the islanders killed so many of their sheep for food, their wool crop was nearly ruined. Without the tweed they weave from the wool, there's only feathers and oil to trade for what they need. Times are still hard from all that slaughter."

Vinnie turned on her heel. Maybe he believed what he was saying, but *she* certainly didn't have to. She would speak to someone in authority, someone like Mr. Powdermaker. He and other rescued adults must be somewhere on this island.

Andrew spoke to her back. "You'll find the boy you call Perry at the manse." It was almost as if Andrew had read her thoughts. "There's been no minister here since I've come, but there's a manse down by the church."

She nodded without turning.

"Remember, you promised not to give me away."

Give him away? He sounded like Grace playing Hide and Seek. "All right," she answered, indulging him.

"And take what clothes you can. Without being seen."

He was raving again. She had best ignore him.

"The children need to be wearing their own things when a boat comes." When she didn't answer, he added softly, "Please. Believe me."

She swung around to confront him one more time, but he was already on his way, the dog at his heels. He didn't take the track, but kept above it, moving swiftly from boulder to boulder until he merged with their lengthening shadows.

six ❧

The children were at the far end of a kind of flagstone walk lying between the cottages and the wall. They were circling as though for a nursery game. They looked peaceful, at home. Vinnie couldn't recognize faces yet, but she had to know who they were. Running toward them, she tried to count: one, two . . . six, seven, eight—no, that was two together—eight and nine . . . So there must be village children there too. Why didn't they have the boat cold?

Dogs trotted to meet Vinnie, then veered off as she pounded along the flagging. The children were just looking up. Grace was the first to break away. With a cry, she flung herself at Vinnie. The next was Lottie, with Joel close behind, shouting Vinnie's name.

"Hush," she warned, hugging them to her. "The people are sick. Oh, Joel, look at you in that little cap. Lottie! I'm so glad to see you all."

"We thought you were dead," Joel told her.

Grace turned on him. "What a thing to say!"

Lottie said, "Where were you? What took you so long?"

"I was sick." Vinnie saw fear and confusion in the faces pressing around her. "I'm all right now," she added, "only tired."

Already she was searching the other faces. Several children held back and stared. Island children, she told herself.

"Promise you'll never leave us again," Grace demanded. "It's awful without you. There's no one to brush my hair. No one to tell stories and show us games."

Vinnie was counting children again. She kept coming out wrong. There were the twins, but was that one Jack? Where was Willie? And what about Nell Haskins? Among the children who stood apart, two seemed on the verge of coming to her. She saw now that Joel was not the only one of her children to be wearing island clothes. For a moment Andrew's plea and warning passed through her mind, but it hardly seemed important while she was still trying to account for everyone.

"Amy and Mabelle," she said, touching the twins' grimy faces. "Jack." She rested her hand on his head. When Toby came back from wherever he was, he would take her to Willie and find Nell.

"Who are these other children?" she asked Lottie and Grace. "Are they your new friends?"

The village children had drawn together—a tight, drab knot of them with the littlest ones nearly hidden by the older ones. Vinnie couldn't help noticing the filthy skin with sores and scabs, wary eyes, greasy hair spiked with dirt.

Grace giggled; she pointed. "Did you forget Nell?"

Vinnie's heart leaped. How could she have missed the little girl? "Nell? Come see me."

Silently Nell pushed through the wall of older children. She had a smaller girl by the hand.

Vinnie knelt down. "I'm very happy to see you again, Nell," she said softly.

Nell looked at her. After a moment she spoke, her voice a whisper. "Are you taking me home?"

Vinnie smiled. "I wish I could. But I'm just like you now. The people here saved us, and now we have to wait for a ship to come and take us away. While we wait, we'll do everything we can to

58

show our gratitude. We won't disturb anyone, and we'll help them any way we can. I'm sure someone's already said all of this to you. To all of you."

Nell shook her head.

Grace said, "We can't understand them. Except her." She indicated the small child whose hand Nell clutched. "She understands them some and us some, but neither very much."

"Who is she?"

Lottie said, "We think her name is Sue, but it might be Lou."

Vinnie turned back to Nell. "Is Sue your special friend?"

Nell's answer was her arm flung around the back of the small child, binding them together.

"Where's Toby?" Vinnie asked them all.

No one answered.

"What's happened to him? Tell me at once."

"Like you?" Lottie suggested.

But Vinnie could see from the blank looks that they had no idea. Maybe he was ill, just as Lottie guessed. He might be recovering in an isolated cottage on another part of the island. Next she asked about Willie.

The faces around her remained closed. Then slowly the children turned to Jack. Amy prodded him. "Please, miss," he said haltingly, "they took him there." He pointed downhill toward the church and manse, toward an enclosure with stones inside it among stands of dock and nettle. "My friend Willie. They didn't say no words over him."

Dead? Buried, and no service? Surely one of the adults would have seen to a proper burial.

"They cried a lot, though," Lottie put in. "They were sorry."

Looking at Jack, Vinnie declared, "We'll do it then. Not today, since I must get back. But soon." They were all so downcast, she searched around for another subject. "Tell me where you are living? Who's taking care of you?"

The twins pointed to one cottage, Jack to another. Grace and

Joel were with separate families. Lottie said, "Every one of us has a sort of mother or father or grandmother. Did you get one too?"

"A very kind lady took care of me. Now she's ill. That's why I can't stay. I need food for her."

Grace said, "Sue gets us bread and things."

Vinnie approached the child. Four or five years old, bundled in island tweed, she had the silent stare of the island children. "Sue?" Vinnie waited for a response. "Is that your name?" The eyes didn't even flicker. "Can you tell your . . . mama that I've come for bread?" The little girl didn't budge.

"Come with me," Joel said. "I can get you bread." He beckoned her into a cottage. A man shuffled out of the inner darkness, the heavy tweed baggy on his thin, bent frame. "He'll give you what you want," Joel assured her.

Vinnie said, "Thank you for taking care of Joel. I am sorry you have all been ill. Peg is ill too."

"Ach, Peig." The man nodded. He coughed.

Joel scooted over to a stone shelf and returned with a round, flat loaf. The man took it from Joel, broke it, and extended half toward Vinnie. She received it with a nod of thanks. The man broke off a small piece from his half and placed it in Joel's mouth. Then, smiling, he caught Joel up in a hug against his side.

After a moment, Joel slipped out of his grasp. "See?" he said. "He likes me. He feeds me. His missus is in bed." He pointed to the bed cupboard.

Vinnie could just make out someone under a blanket. She said to the man, "I can take Joel back with me, and then you'll have less bother."

The man smiled and nodded, but as soon as she took Joel's hand and began to lead him out, the man blocked them with surprising swiftness. His face broke out in moisture. From the bed cupboard, the woman groaned. Straightening, the man pointed down to Joel and shook his head.

"All right," Vinnie said. "But I'll be back for him."

She told the children that too. "Soon," she promised. She was growing anxious about Peg. When the sun set, she might have trouble finding her way back across the island.

Just as she waved good-bye, a girl about Vinnie's age came out of a cottage with a bottle. "Peig," she said. Vinnie looked at the label, which said Godfrey's Cordial. Probably it was a strengthening tonic. A woman poked her face out the door and croaked an order at the girl. She hiked her skirt and scrambled behind the cottage and over a garden wall. In a moment she was back with a bunch of loose cabbage leaves, which she placed in Vinnie's basket.

The village dogs followed Vinnie for a while, then turned back. It felt lonely on the path with the darkness drawing in, turning the sea dull and lumpy, transforming the barren hillside into crouching black masses of stones and hillocks. Next time, she thought, she would go to Perry. Probably he knew where everyone else was. She would show Andrew how wrong he was about the islanders.

She was growing tired. She tripped over stones and sometimes stumbled from the path. Night came so swiftly that the horizon shrank before her eyes. She shifted the basket with its bottle and greens and bread. The wind's icy fingers raked her and thrust her on. She began to run.

She ran until her legs and chest and throat ached. Then, suddenly quite near, solid and low, the cottage loomed. She raced over to it only to discover that it was one of the little round huts. She staggered back to the path, but the path had gone. Sobbing, she plunged headlong down the slope. She couldn't see at all. She couldn't stop either.

Then she ran full tilt into something that knocked her sideways. Winded, she staggered, pitched forward. But her fall was checked. She was eased down.

61

"Are you a bird then? Have you wings?"

She couldn't utter a word. She just took in the sound of Andrew's voice.

When the two of them started back up the hill, she groaned. Why was every place you had to get to around here uphill?

"We're almost there," he told her.

"So I was heading right."

"It only takes a little bit of wrong here to be the death of you. You can't go running after dark. You must mind the time. As I do."

"I can't. I have nothing to tell time with."

"Keep your eyes open and you'll learn. I have. Today is the first time I've missed low tide. Mind, it doesn't matter for the sheep. There's scant tending of them this time of year. When they fetched you from the sea, I was put out there and told to pull grass for the sheep. I expect the islanders only wanted to keep me from you, for the sheep can get their own grass."

Turning downhill, they came to the cottage.

"If she's asleep," he whispered, "I'll come for a moment. I looked in before. I thought there might be a cup of broth. There was no sound from her then."

"Is that why you were up there when you stopped me?"

He nodded. "I went looking. Then I heard you running. I came crosswise to catch you up."

Vinnie sighed. "I'm glad," she told him softly. What did it matter if he was given to fancies and imagined plots against him? He had saved her from dashing over the cliff.

Inside the cottage she stood stock-still. Peg was asleep. Andrew slipped past her. He seemed at ease in the dark. Trying to follow, she discovered to her amazement that she knew her way around too. Here was the table, there the stone shelf.

Andrew stirred the fire into life. Soon a small flame was flicking its tongue this way and that. Andrew retreated. She guessed he was fetching more turf. She glanced toward Peg, who still slept. Andrew returned. He knelt at the fire. The flame sputtered, then licked itself into shape and settled back onto the stones.

She handed him the oil bag and watched him fill the lamp and light it. Together they looked over the bread and greens. "Kale," Andrew whispered. "You boil it with birds or with sowans."

"With what?"

"The meal. But don't use much. They don't have enough to last the season." He set the pot with the soaking carcasses over the flame and lowered the chain to speed the cooking. Then, to her dismay, he took the pot from the hook, carried it to the door, and emptied the water over the wind wall. After that, he refilled the pot and set it back to cook.

Later she understood why he had thrown the first water away. This broth wasn't so salty or fishy as the first batch she had brewed. As soon as Andrew drank some and broke off a piece of bannock, he walked quietly to the door. Vinnie followed him. He could sleep there by the door. She would give him a shawl for covering. But he insisted that he would be better off waiting for the next low tide in one of the little huts, one of the cleits. He would accept her skirt, though, to throw across his shoulders.

Quickly, with hardly a thought for tomorrow, Vinnie scurried back in and pulled off her skirt. She groped around and found Peg's heavy skirt, put it on, and carried her own back to Andrew, who had crouched down inside the wind wall to wait. Without a word, he took the skirt and disappeared.

Back she went, feeling the weight and scratchiness of Peg's garment. When Peg finally woke up and saw Vinnie, she reached out with quivering fingers, touching Vinnie's brow, speaking softly, with wonderment. Vinnie guessed that Peg, waking earlier, had been frightened by Vinnie's long absence.

Vinnie brought the bottle of Godfrey's Cordial to the bed cupboard. After a few sips, Peg nodded. She was able to take a whole cupful of broth now. Vinnie smiled with relief. Peg, warmed and eased, held the smile and then gave it back to Vinnie, her face aglow.

In the days that followed, Vinnie used any excuse to go outside. She scrubbed the table and the stone shelves, going back and forth to the spring for water. She kept watching for Andrew. She wished she had mentioned cleanliness to Lottie, who could at least keep the little ones presentable.

Presentable to whom? That brought Vinnie up short. Well, the others from the ship. Hoping to come across some sign of them, she explored a little farther each day. Over the hill, beyond the storage huts that Andrew called cleits, she came to a deep valley where sheep flocked. As soon as they saw her they started blatting. Some came toward her and bawled, while the light glinted across their yellow eyes and steam rolled from their gaping mouths.

She walked all the way around the rim of the valley, until she was so close to the cliffs she felt suddenly giddy. Remembering her headlong plunge in the dark, she crouched low. It took a moment before she dared look down at the rocks, the wind-whipped sea. Today it twinkled like chips of blue glass, vicious and radiant.

Could a ship ride safely over water like that? At the docks in Liverpool, she had heard someone speaking of sea routes and shipping lanes. Mr. Powdermaker had assured Mrs. Stott that the *Roger F. Laing* was scheduled to travel one of the most direct lanes. Vinnie had imagined the sea marked out neatly for different kinds of ships, the fast steamers taking the outside lanes, the slower sailing packets confined to the inside. Fields were harvested in that fashion, the horse teams surging ahead, the people with scythes moving at a slower pace on the inside rows.

Vinnie gazed out to sea. How did they know where those shipping lanes were? How could you mark out a sea route through tumbling waves? Were Mr. and Mrs. Stott directing search boats from North America or from England?

Carefully Vinnie retraced her steps. The slopes were still green inside the vales. Grazing sheep scattered before her, then dropped their heads to the lush grass once more. Yet winter must be well along now. Christmas had come and gone without her knowing it. How much longer would she have to wait before finding adults from the ship? When would Andrew return?

Coming back to the cottage, she decided that Peg was well enough now to be left for a while. Tomorrow Vinnie would go to the village. But when she woke the next day and quickly dressed, Peg insisted on getting herself ready as well. Snow had fallen overnight, and Peg was fretting and anxious. Vinnie tried to keep her from the weather, but Peg seemed determined to go somewhere, and Vinnie had no choice but to go with her.

In spite of Peg's weakness, she took the slope at a pace that turned Vinnie breathless. All the long way up and then over to the rim of the valley, Vinnie straggled after the woman, who carried a jug, hiked her heavy skirt, and plodded on with purpose.

When Vinnie first looked down, she thought the sheep had gone. The clumps of sedge and heather and the rocks scarcely showed beneath the snow. With hardly any voice, Peg spoke into that seemingly empty white basin and called it to life. Lumps of snow rose and cracked and parted. Then they fell away, became standing sheep, all heads pointed toward Peg.

She spoke again. One of them humped through the snow like a seal on the beach. Peg started toward it, but stumbled. Drifts had collected; she wasn't strong enough to wade through. When the sheep reached her, Peg probed under the ewe's hindquarters. Now Vinnie knew where the milk had come from. Sheep's milk! Peg, her arm resting across the sheep's back, turned to Vinnie with a look of clear rebuke. Then, puffing audibly, Peg left the sheep and headed for the nearest cleit.

Peg must intend to bring back some of the salted birds. To spare her, Vinnie lurched ahead. When she stooped to duck under the fan of snow that spread from the thatch, the whole snow canopy slid down onto her head and back. She squealed. Peg let out a yelp of laughter. Through the blur of snow, Vinnie saw Peg with her head thrown back, and for an instant she was not Peg anymore. Snow and laughter and ribbons of black all rushed across Vinnie's vision. She saw a woman, a black bear of a woman, rocking on her heels and slapping her skirt. It was wet and cold, but the laughter spread through Vinnie like warmth.

Reaching into the cleit for a few of the birds and bunching them inside her skirt, Vinnie went on with Peg, who was beginning to stagger now, to falter. Vinnie was alarmed. She hauled Peg down the last slope and led her inside before the fire and tucked a blanket around her. What a worry people could be. Grown-up people, that is. You couldn't boss them the way you could little children, and that left you nowhere at all with them.

There wasn't much Godfrey's Cordial left. Vinnie poured some into a spoon. Peg reached for it, her trembling fingers gripping Vinnie's arm. "Aah," she sighed, closing her eyes with relief. She began to breathe more easily. She kept hold of Vinnie's sleeve, tugging a little, nodding. Vinnie helped her to her feet and into the bed cupboard.

The wind came up. All that day and the following night, the snow was driven first one way, then another, until drifts closed in around the cottage. Then a stinging rain fell. It froze the snow in solid swirls. Ramparts of ice reared up from the wind wall. After that, the wind couldn't alter the shapes it had carved out of the snow. Beyond the white hillside Vinnie could see the black water and the silvered stacks and islands. Nothing on land stirred. There was no call, no bleat, no living sound.

Peg felt better. She melted water and stirred the meal into it for sowans. She spun yarn with increasing deftness, her tense fingers tugging the thread with urgency while she squinted out over the icy landscape and yearned toward the distance, toward things out there she could not reach. Vinnie guessed that Peg was worried about the sheep.

66

First thing each morning, Vinnie hurried to the door to look for the sun. But day after day, thick, dull clouds hung over the white land.

Peg showed Vinnie how to drop a spindle and pull a thread from the fleece. The gray wool reminded her of the clouds; the white wool looked pretty and unreal. Peg hung the skeins of yarn, matching color to color. The semicircle dangling over the fire was like the Christmas crown at the Stotts'—a splendid wreath made of evergreen branches, with candles standing up from it in a circle of light, and mistletoe and ribbons hanging down. The ribbons had gifts attached to them.

Vinnie's first sight of it had taken her breath away. Grace and Joel, dazzled for an instant, had raced to it, demanding to know which ribbons were theirs to tug. Mrs. Stott had warned them that if they were too rough, they would jounce the candles and hot tallow would drop on them. But Mr. Stott had laughed away all caution. While he steadied the green crown of lights, Grace and Joel had chased and run with yellow and red ribbons wrapped around their fingers, pouncing on a bag of boiled sweets that each one claimed, until a walnut came tumbling down with a sugar-plum inside the shell.

There had been a present for Vinnie too that Christmas eve, a book called *The Heroes.* But, oh, the thrill of that Christmas crown. Clutching her knees, Vinnie rocked to and fro, remembering. For the colored ribbons hanging from the pungent evergreen had struck in her such longing that at first she had scarcely noticed the book, even though Mr. Stott himself placed it in her hands.

In the dim cottage, the skeins of yarns could almost be ribbons, elusive as shadows in the firelight. What else with those shadows? The scent of the green boughs. Snow and laughter. Sweetness. Still hugging her knees and rocking, Vinnie pictured houses with stairs and chests of drawers and beds, with shelves for books, and lamps with chimneys and shades, with windows to let in the light and mirrors to hold it. Like the gilt-framed mirror in the Stotts' drawing room.

Faces you couldn't look at closely without seeming rude could be secretly examined within that golden frame. Vinnie used to stand aside, ready to take Joel's hand if needed, and see first one person and then another, until they became people in a story she was telling.

When sometimes a strange face gazed out from the mirror, Vinnie supposed she herself must have put it there. Once it appeared in a black bonnet when no one in the room was dressed in black. Another time it came laughing out at her with such gusto she almost laughed in return.

Vinnie looked past the shadows. There was Peg, who had hovered over her when she was sick and laughed at her in the snow. But how could you picture a person before you ever met her? Besides, there had been that bonnet, ribbons pulling it snug under the chin. Who, then, if not Peg? Vinnie dropped her face to her knees.

seven 🌱

Late at night the wind died altogether. Inside the cottage things creaked as if waking from a long sleep. Vinnie could just hear the rope inside the door, the hook and chain over the hearth. The plunger leaned against the empty churn, and a sheepskin, not yet cured, scraped like a timid, living animal at the wall where it hung. The house crouched stiff and cold.

By morning the clouds had thinned enough for a little brightness to filter through the gray mass. The roof sent down tiny transparent shoots. Vinnie watched them grow. They had all the colors of the Christmas crown and more. The glassy spines dripped as the heat from the fire moved out to them. Vinnie reached. At her touch, an icicle slid from its stem and shattered.

Vinnie spun around. It was almost as if she had broken one of the treasures of the house, but Peg, who was winding a skein of yarn, didn't even look up. In a sudden, murderous sweep, Vinnie mowed down a swathe of the icicles. Falling, they sounded like chimes. This time Peg sent Vinnie an inquiring look. Vinnie flung herself back inside.

She was poking around, looking for something different to do, when Peg rose suddenly and waved her silent. Something was approaching. Something making a lot of noise. Vinnie thought even a frost giant would be welcome if it broke this awful monotony.

A dog trotted in through the door and faced them expectantly. It had huge ice balls on its paws; it was shivering so violently the water shot out from it like spray.

"Kep!" Vinnie cried. Hoping her naming hadn't betrayed Andrew, she grabbed an empty sack and began to rub the dog furiously. Surely Andrew would appear any moment now and free her from pretense.

But there was no Andrew, and as she worked away on the freezing dog, she began to wonder whether Andrew was in some kind of trouble. She glanced at Peg, who was staring down at her. Or was it at the dog? The next thing Vinnie knew, Peg was binding her feet in sacks. She was getting ready to go out on the ice. She straightened long enough to gesture briefly at Vinnie. Bundle up, the gesture commanded. Hurry, it said quite clearly.

Peg took down the coil of rope by the door. She hesitated, scowled, and ducked back into the corner, from which she emerged with something that looked like a net made of stems and roots.

Being ready was one thing. Getting anywhere over the ice was quite another. Kep started right off, his feet skidding out from under him but somehow propelling him forward. His feet clicked as he clawed to keep his footing. Peg went back inside and returned with a small reaping hook for Vinnie, a knife for herself, and two more sacks. These she folded. She sat down on one and slid the other to Vinnie. Down, she beckoned. Sit down.

In the next moment they were on their way, braking themselves as often as they could with knife or hook. Every time they came close to an ice-sheathed rock they would grab for it, but it was hard to hold on to anything. Their fingers slipped over the island's armor.

Down they went, slowing only enough to control their direc-

70

tion. Kep was sliding too. What would keep him from falling off the cliff?

Vinnie called to him. He managed to turn, but he kept on sliding backward. She gave herself a mighty thrust and went sailing down to him. The slope was a blur. She could hear Peg shout. She could hear her own breath shrill in her throat. She was abreast of him now.

Time to slow down. She plunged the hook sideways and out, but the curved blade scraped across the surface. She pulled in her legs and swiveled onto her stomach. The hook was flailing at the air, at an ice hill, and now at something protruding under the shell of snow and ice. She grabbed and held on. The sacking continued on by itself until it disappeared over the cliff. Meanwhile Kep, still sliding, glanced against her shoulder. She swung her legs out just as Toby had done in the sea. She felt the dog's claws through her skirt, clutching.

"Oh, Kep," she breathed, flinging one arm down to grab him at the neck. Her arms were trembling. She just held tight until Peg came to a halt beside her and delivered a rapid sermon on the foolishness of risking one's life for an animal, not a word of which Vinnie could translate, though the message was perfectly clear.

When the tirade was over, Peg set to work opening the net and pulling the dog's legs through the bottom of it. She pinned the knife through it while she tied on the rope. Now they were ready to go. But slowly, she insisted, wagging a finger at Vinnie and going "Whsssht" to remind her what she must never do again.

Vinnie nodded obediently. She couldn't help smiling, though. As if she wanted to spin down this slope for fun!

It wasn't far to the cliff's edge, where Kep had been leading them. The trouble was that the cliff overhung the ledges beneath it. Vinnie could see no way to get down. Was Andrew stuck somewhere underneath them? It was hard to creep to the edge and peer over.

Peg was letting out rope. She glanced out into the channel, then concentrated on her rope. The channel? Vinnie hadn't looked that far. Now she did. She saw Andrew standing on ice. Only the boulders that strewed the channel kept the ice floe from the current. She could see at once that if the ice melted or turned, it would slip between the rocks. Already, it had broken off from a sheet that extended like a bridge to the shore.

Peg carved deep ruts in the cliff. She drew Vinnie's hands to her waist. Vinnie began to realize what Peg intended; the dog would be let down with a rope for Andrew. Vinnie reached around Peg so that one freezing hand gripped the other. Peg leaned over the cliff, her toes in the ruts as she thrust the netted dog out over the drop. Vinnie couldn't bear to watch Kep dangling in space, but she could feel the exact moment Peg checked his fall, for her whole body jerked. Vinnie held on with all her might. Then Peg let out rope; the tension in her back and arms eased. She glided back, and Vinnie slid off to one side.

Far below, Kep, looking small and clumsy in the net, clambered over rocks, spashed in the channel, broke through ice, and then clung to a rock. Finally there was only one stretch of swirling black water between him and Andrew. Though Vinnie couldn't hear any voice, she could see that Andrew was calling him. Surely Kep would drown in that current with the net ensnaring him.

She saw him leap. He disappeared at once. Andrew plunged in after him. For what seemed an eternity, he groped and flailed, but it could only have taken a minute or so before the rope twanged and sent its first shock wave up toward Peg. "Pull, pull," Vinnie cried, but Peg sat motionless, all her attention on the channel. With the next twanging, she began to draw the rope very slowly into coils. *Back,* her body told Vinnie, as Andrew and Kep rolled onto the rock.

Once Kep was free, he scampered away along the headland. Moments later he was with Vinnie and Peg on the cliff, shivering again but very much alive.

72

It took a long time to pull Andrew up. Slowly, slowly the coil grew. Then Kep's tail began to wave. He rose to his feet, backed off, and crouched once more.

Andrew climbed the last bit, letting Peg take his hand and Vinnie grab his baggy trousers to roll him up onto the cliff. In an instant, Peg slipped off her homespun skirt, swiveled, then worked Andrew out of his jacket and vest. A quick gesture with her head, chin leading, sent Vinnie to Andrew's feet. She tugged the soaked tweed while Peg held him by the shoulders. It was a good thing those trousers were so large, but it was hard work anyway. The salt stung her hands, and the cold air made her fingers ache as she grasped the cloth.

As soon as Vinnie had pulled the trousers free, Peg tossed the skirt to her, and she brought the waist up around his feet. After that, Andrew took over. His teeth chattered so hard he couldn't speak, but he pulled up the skirt. Peg worked to remove his shirt. Vinnie untied her shawl and threw that over Andrew. Then Peg started to rub him.

"Kep," Andrew said.

Vinnie scrubbed the dog with the hem of her skirt. Andrew began to take some deep breaths.

A fine rain was falling. It came on warming airs and clung to the ice, softening its surface. It made climbing back uphill possible, though there were still slick spots that resisted toeholds. It was slow, exhausting work.

They all but fell into the cottage. Vinnie was amazed at Peg's stamina. First she pulled on a ragged homespun dress; then she threw some ice into the pot and started it boiling. Next she took Andrew's things from the net and spread them to dry. It would take forever, thought Vinnie. Poor Andrew would have to stay dressed like a woman.

Vinnie worked at her wet shoes, which were stiff and torn. Finally her feet were free. She leaned back on her elbows and stuck her toes up to the fire. Outside the fine rain hissed as it fell;

inside sluggish black drops ran down the walls and turned the edges of the floor to mud.

As soon as Andrew was warmed with broth, Peg railed at him. When Andrew tried to say something, her words just rode right over his. Vinnie asked him if he understood Peg.

"Not everything." Then he added quickly, "And mind, she doesn't know I've crossed anywhere else. She thinks this was the only time, on the ice."

During this exchange, Peg had fallen silent. Now she sipped her broth and eyed the two of them.

"She doesn't like us speaking English together," Vinnie murmured. "Talk to her."

In halting phrases, Andrew said something to Peg that prompted her to shoot back a reply. He pressed on. Finally she grunted, satisfied.

"What did you say?"

"That I was thinking of her sheep. Thinking they'd need to be helped."

"That was clever."

"It was true."

"Well, you can't do anything about them now until your clothes dry."

"We'll have to. The sheep in the valley will be starving."

Peg, who was beginning to complain agin, went to the nearly empty meal sack. Whatever she said brought a quick smile and a brief reply from Andrew. He told Vinnie that Peg was cross with her because she hadn't milked the sheep during all the time Peg lay sick. The sheep had no milk now.

"How was I to know?" Vinnie demanded.

Andrew shrugged. "These islanders think we ought to be just like them."

"Besides, the sheep wouldn't let me near. And I don't know how to milk."

Andrew laughed. "She told me. She says you're ignorant, but

you are like the bird of spring and have lightened her heart. She says since she cannot have a son, you will do for a daughter. You must learn to be a sheep woman like her. At least until you marry."

Let him tease, Vinnie thought. Just wait till they went out to the sheep together, he in his skirt. He'd think twice before he made fun of her again.

But she had no breath to spare for taunts that day. It took all their energy and the remaining hours of daylight to carry a sack of barley to the vale and dig out the sheep. Vinnie, who was supposed to sprinkle the barley a little at a time, was nearly mobbed by the starving animals. Flocked and contained in the valley, they had eaten dirt and the wool off each other's backs. Freed finally, they would trample anything and anyone to get to food.

Three of the sheep, too weak to survive out there, had to be pulled over the snow crust and dragged down the hill to the cottage. There they were fed gruel and bird oil, but one refused to swallow. Vinnie, certain that it was on the verge of death, dribbled Godfrey's Cordial into its cold mouth until the sheep began to swallow, to open its eyes. Time for gruel. And that went down too.

Peg was horrified when she saw what Vinnie had done with the precious medicine. But Andrew thought Vinnie showed every sign of making a first-class sheep woman. "You'll do for a daughter," he told her. "You'll do for Peg." And he went on to explain that since Peg was a widow without a son, she had only feathers and oil to trade to the tacksman in the spring. Without a man to weave, she made up for the lack of tweed by tending the main flock.

"Only the men weave?"

"Exactly. And there aren't enough of them. That's why they'll be calling me to a loom before long."

"Can you really weave?"

Andrew nodded. "My granddad still does a bit of weaving. When he came to live with us, he brought his loom. Some people prize the homespun cloth, even with the mills coming everywhere. It's from him I started learning, though the island looms are not the same as his. I've had to set myself to study the island ways. It's just like with their words. What I knew from my granddad has helped me understand island speech, but still I must pick up what I can. It's not easy. The littlest children are best at it, but then they forget their own language as well."

"Forget English? Surely not!"

Andrew gave her a look. "Have you tried talking with the girl or the little boys? Of course, Jamie was only a baby in arms when we came. But I'll wager the others spoke English then."

Vinnie tried to picture them there on the village street, but the only new face she could recall belonged to Nell's friend Sue—or Lou. Vinnie sighed. She was too tired to think about it now.

Four birds were cooked that evening, two for Andrew, and one each for Vinnie and Peg. Andrew gave much to Kep, who gulped down meat and bones together, then went off to a corner to regurgitate it all and consume it again with proper chewing and crunching. Neither Peg nor Andrew paid any attention to this performance. They were trying to speak together, planning what to do for the sheep in the vale. Seaweed, he told Vinnie. Seaweed tomorrow. Then his head dropped forward and he spoke no more.

Peg watched him for a moment. She beckoned Vinnie. Together they carried Andrew, his heavy skirt trailing on the dirt floor, and settled him in the bed cupboard. Then they pulled the straw-filled sacks apart to make two separate beds on the floor. Peg banked the fire and extinguished the lamp.

The cottage had never been like this before, the three sheep giving off a strong smell and heat and moisture, their eyes gleaming yellow in the dark.

Facedown in the bed cupboard, Andrew snored lightly.

Pulling her shawl up to her ears, Vinnie squirmed and nestled

76

on her sack. Something collapsed against her back. She turned her head just enough to see that Kep had flung himself beside her. She inched over to give him a little more space. He filled it at once, sprawling with a groan of satisfaction, legs up, his muzzle seeking the crook of her neck and then going slack.

The next day they beat a path down the incline at the headland, and at low tide gathered rockweed for the sheep. Vinnie noticed that Andrew avoided looking out toward his island. He averted his eyes from the rocks that stretched out like paving stones in the shallows. Surely Peg must realize that Andrew could make it across at dead low, but she too seemed to look the other way.

They hauled the seaweed up in the net bag and in the basket. Vinnie's hands stung, even afterward, even at night. The skin reddened and cracked and would not heal.

It was better when the snow began to melt and they could pull grass for the sheep. When she went foraging with Andrew, he talked about the sheep on the little island. They had scattered at the storm's onset and so would have fared better than the ones gathered in the vale. But there was no way to check on them without revealing his escape route.

When the three weak sheep were put out of the house, they took themselves onto the roof where they began to nibble the ropes of woven stems that held down the thatch. Vinnie and Andrew pelted them with snowballs and finally had to send Kep up top to keep the roof from being eaten.

During the foraging, Andrew talked about his granddad, who used to keep sheep and was a master weaver. He talked about his brothers and his father, who was a printer, and his mother, who worked in the print shop too, and about his uncle who went to America to become a railroad man in Buffalo, New York, and then bought a printing press and sent for one of his nephews to join him. Sent for Andrew.

Early one morning Andrew told Vinnie, "I dreamed I was there, in Buffalo." They were just stirring, although Peg was already outside.

Vinnie couldn't help asking what it was like, in spite of her doubts about the existence of such a place.

"I don't know." Andrew yawned and stretched. Kep came padding to him and leaned against his knee. "Real. Exactly what I expected."

"Was your uncle there? I mean, in the dream."

"Yes, and the street where he lives and the railroad depot. All of it." Andrew rubbed his eyes.

"That would be because your uncle described it so well."

Andrew nodded, but he was scowling too. "I've had so many dreams since I've been here." He sat with his chin in his hands, his eyes downcast.

Peg had returned. She settled in the doorway with her knitting. Vinnie picked up her work too. They would eat nothing yet, for their two meals had to hold them through the long dark night. Breakfast would be put off until midday when they came inside, cold and wet.

To get his mind off Buffalo, Vinnie asked him about the little island. He talked about the earth house that was built right into the grassy hill, huge upright slabs for cornerstones and lintel, and stone paving on the floor. There was another like it on the outermost island; the islanders called it the giant's house. In the spring the girls and young women had to be the first ones inside. Later, anyone out on the island for eggs or fowl could shelter there or store their catch along with food and sheepskins always kept on hand. No one ever wintered on that island because of the distance and the treacherous rocks surrounding it; yet the islanders still provided for the unforeseen.

"The giant's house," said Vinnie. "I'm glad you didn't have to live in it."

"Well, there are no sheep on that island. Anyway, living

in either earth house is supposed to give you strength, manhood."

Vinnie smiled. "Then by the time you get to your uncle, you'll be a man. Won't he be pleased?"

Andrew shrugged. "By now, probably one of my brothers has gone instead."

"Even so," Vinnie insisted, "you'll get there too." She wondered what it would be like landing in a strange city. She could never have managed in Liverpool without Mrs. Stott. Alone, she would have been swallowed up in the frantic crowds she had seen being rushed along the streets. Mrs. Stott's carriage had passed shipping agents and brokers, provision shops and eating houses and drinking vaults, until suddenly it was blocked by hundreds of emigrants being shoved and dragged like cattle to market. "Animals," the driver had called them as he turned off the main thoroughfare. "Best leave them to the man-catchers." That was what he called the runners and emigration agents.

"My uncle arranged everything," Andrew went on. "I was to be met by an agent in New York who would see that I kept my box, for there are men like the runners in Liverpool and Glasgow who'll take all your possessions. You must follow them or lose everything. And then you're charged a frightful sum for lodgings. My uncle says they are in league with the lodging-house keepers. He saw to it that I'd have no such worry and would be sent promptly on my way." Andrew sighed. "I wonder what he thought when I never came."

"But he would have been told," Vinnie exclaimed. "They're all connected, Liverpool and New York and other places. Mr. Powdermaker says so." But she was thinking that Andrew had just confirmed her worst fears: New York or Halifax might be no better than Liverpool.

"They must believe me dead," Andrew said.

Vinnie leaned toward him. "Think of the surprise then."

"After all this time . . . ?"

Vinnie said, "It will be all right. You're not alone anymore. You'll be fine now."

He thought a moment. "Maybe," he said. "I suppose there's a better chance." He paused. "But none of you know the islanders. They're crafty."

Vinnie snorted. "Peg, crafty?"

"You don't know them," he said again.

"But I will soon. Could you tell Peg that I must go to the village to see my children? The snow ought to be gone enough now."

Andrew nodded. "I expect she'll go with you, though. There's no more milking now, no more cheese till spring. She'll want to keep an eye on you, Vinnie. She won't think of losing you."

Vinnie didn't try to argue. If he was bound to see himself as captive, all she could do was reassure him about their future rescue. She cast off the last row of the stocking she had just completed. Laying it beside its mate, she glanced up to see what Peg thought of this accomplishment. Peg, her needles clicking, smiled and nodded. She spoke a few words to Andrew meant for Vinnie.

"Next pair's your own," Andrew interpreted. "You'll need woolen stockings on your feet under sackcloth; your shoes are too torn to wear to the village through the snow."

"We're going?" Vinnie exclaimed. "She knew! Did you tell her?"

Andrew shook his head. "She heard us, though. She didn't need the words."

Vinnie scrambled to her feet and ran to the doorway. "Oh, thank you," she said, "thank you."

Peg's needles went still. She gave Vinnie a searching look. Her knitting in one hand, with the other she smoothed back a strand of Vinnie's hair. For a moment the hand remained, just resting against Vinnie's cheek. Then Peg resumed her knitting. Vinnie's own hand went to her face; she could feel Peg's touch like a blessing.

80

eight 🦋

Peg's sure stride carried her easily over concealed rocks and through pools of melted snow. But Vinnie wasn't used to walking with her feet bound in sacks. Wads of felted wool protected her soles and kept her new stockings fairly dry. But she felt a little awkward. She hoped the children would be with her when she called on Master Perry so that he might not notice the strange foot garb.

As she slapped down into the street, there was such a din coming from the cottages that the village sounded, of all things, like Liverpool. Yet there stood women in the feeble sun, knitting and spinning together as if nothing were amiss. Only where were the children?

Vinnie peered in at the first door she came to. After a moment, she made out the figure of a man seated on at stool at a loom. The shuttle flew back and forth as he yanked and banged in a kind of frenzy. The clatter never let up, not for an instant.

As Vinnie went on along the street, the racket mounted. She could see—but not hear—the women greet Peg, who had dressed with care this day, a white fringe at the front of her headkerchief. Most of the women wore the same kind of fringes, like uniforms. They made much of Peg, and she made much of one who would soon have a baby. When Vinnie came up to them, they all turned to greet her too.

Peg took in Vinnie's searching look, questioned the women, and set Vinnie toward the pathway that led out of the village. As soon as she was away from the loom racket, she started calling. But it was Perry, not Grace or Joel or Lottie, who appeared around the side of the church.

With a cry, she ran toward him. "Master Perry!"

He folded his arms at her coming and stepped back. "Vinnie? I almost didn't know you, dressed like that."

Stopping short, she glanced down at herself, then at him. He was wearing his own clothes. They were rumpled and stained, but he carried them with an air that proclaimed his station. She noticed too that his shoes were hardly worn. She told him that it was good to find him looking so well.

"Really?" he answered. "Even though last time we were together you nearly killed me?"

She was baffled until she remembered the accident with the boat hook. Did he think she had swatted him to keep him off the crate?

"I understand you dragged me up afterward," he went on, "you and a boy. Gave me your places. I'll remember that when I report it."

"Aren't you glad to see me?" she whispered.

"Glad to see the nursery maid parading about like one of the island savages?"

"I'll be on my way," she said, her face burning. "I'm looking for the children."

"They're on the beach. Digging shellfish like navvies. The Ragged School children with my sister and brother, all dressed alike in that rough cloth."

Vinnie said, "The homespun is more suitable here. It keeps you warm and dry."

82

"I know nothing of homespun." He stood there, looking cold and sour and unhappy.

"Have you seen Toby?" she asked.

"Who?"

"The boy who— Don't you remember Toby?"

"There's no one with me but a crippled old man who brings the food. I've seen no other passengers from the ship, only a herd boy who says he's off a different wreck. I'm quite alone."

Vinnie nodded. She went on down the path, past two rowing boats weighted with rocks and all the way to the gravelly strand. The children were out toward the headland. When she called, heads popped up, hands shielded eyes. All of her group charged toward her except Nell, who remained among the other children. Vinnie ran too, stumbling over her foot wrappings, beyond caring what she looked like, her arms wide, embracing.

After his hug, Joel danced up and down. "We had such snow. They haven't sleds here. Can I have my overshoes?"

Grace still clutched her hand. "We went to church. I don't know if it was church. It took a long time and the hymn was awful loud."

"It's where Perry is," Joel explained. "The real house next door. With a real stove. Do you think that's fair?"

Jack spoke softly. "I liked it when they sang."

The other children came along as Vinnie's group dragged her toward a pile of drift they were gathering. Grace ran to a girl around Vinnie's age. "This is my friend," she told Vinnie.

Vinnie smiled at the girl, the one who had brought her the kale. "What's her name?"

"I'm not sure. It might be Thora." At this, the girl caught Grace up in a hug.

"I'm glad you have a friend," Vinnie said, "but don't forget your brother needs you too."

"Joel has a grandmama now and a grandpapa."

Vinnie nodded. She turned to Nell, who, keeping her distance, stared up at Vinnie. Vinnie noticed a basket full of mussels the children had pried from the ebb tide. She said, "How would you like to teach your friends one of our games?"

Joel jumped beside her. "And then when it's teatime you'll tell us a story."

"They don't have teatime," Grace snapped at him.

Vinnie said quickly, "We'll pretend a tea party, and of course I'll tell you a story." She caught a look from Lottie, a kind of glower. "What's wrong with that?" she asked.

"Then you'll go away again," Lottie grumbled.

Maybe not, thought Vinnie, wondering how she could manage to stay with them. She scooped up a handful of mussels and gave one to each child. But when she tried to distribute the next handful beyond her little cluster of children, the others didn't know what to do. "It's a game," she told them resolutely. "You watch us; then you can play too."

The older girl who was Grace's friend took a mussel from Vinnie and carefully set it back in the basket.

Vinnie took a long stone and, with the tip of it, drew a circle. She placed seven mussels in its center. "Now," she exclaimed, "who wants to go first?"

Joel did. He flung his mussel at the heap; it bounced once and grounded in the sand. Grace was next. She couldn't move any of the mussels, even though she managed to strike them. "Lottie?"

Lottie threw hers with a sudden lunge. Her mussel scattered the others and sent two flipping out of the circle. "I'm ahead!" she declared, and flashed the island children a look of challenge. Jack beat her, though, with three mussels over the line.

"I want another turn," cried Joel.

Lottie pushed him back. "Not yet. And don't smudge the line."

The twins were shy about playing. They didn't throw their mussels, only dropped them.

By now the village children had closed around the circle. One

84

reached out to Vinnie. Quickly she popped her mussel into his hand. He threw it, losing his own but gaining another that skipped out over the line. The other children pressed forward. Vinnie passed out mussels to all who held out their hands. The game went on around the circle, island children and Vinnie's children, one after another. Only the very youngest didn't play, the youngest and Nell and her inseparable companion, Sue-Lou. But they watched. And every time Vinnie exclaimed at a good throw, Nell's eyes fastened on her face and drank in the laughter and praise.

On their way uphill to the village, Jack slipped in between Joel and Vinnie and touched her skirt. "Please, miss." He pointed to the church and manse. "The words for Willie?"

"I haven't forgotten," she told him.

As soon as he moved away, Grace and Joel fell in step beside her. She swung their hands. "Now, we're out for a walk," she said to them. "Where shall we go? Who shall we see?"

"The muffin man," Grace decided.

"The muffin man!" shouted Joel over the racket of the looms.

Vinnie propelled the two children toward Peg. "Grace," she said. "Joel. This is Peg."

Joel's bow made all the women laugh. The one who was going to have a baby spoke softly, briefly touching Joel's head. Then they all fell silent.

Joel ran to a doorway where another woman emerged from the clatter and dusty closeness. She opened her arms for Joel, who walked straight into them. Turning within the hug, he said, "This is Fan. I think she's my grandmama."

"Oh, no," Vinnie started to object. But the woman was smiling so warmly, Vinnie had to swallow her protest and smile in return.

It troubled her, though, that impulse to deny, to protect the children from false claims on them. It meant she had begun to believe Andrew, just a little anyhow. She would have to guard against such nonsense. These people were simply doing what any decent folk would do. And more than that, they were giving the castaway children a home until they could be returned to their own places and people.

It became clear to Vinnie that Peg was not planning to return to her cottage that day. Two older boys were sent out of the village on an errand in that direction, but Vinnie didn't take much notice of them. She was trying to find a quiet place to take the little ones for their pretend tea. Grace brought bannock and cheese. Like the village dogs, the children wandered in and out of cottages, and there seemed to be no regular mealtimes.

They ended sitting inside a kale plot with a stone wall at their backs. The bannock and cheese were shared; it was time for a story. Vinnie chose her favorite one from *The Heroes*, about the good ship *Argo* stuck in the sand. She tried to cut it short, but Grace remembered the parts she left out. "Sing the magic song," she demanded. "The song Orpheus sang to make the boat go."

"The song," echoed Joel.

" 'How sweet it is to ride upon the surges,' " Vinnie began, with a lilt that was almost singing, " 'and to leap from wave to wave. . . .' " Grace nodded with contentment. Joel leaned against her. " 'How sweet it is to roam across the ocean, and see new towns and wondrous lands, and to come home laden with treasure, and to win undying fame!' And the good ship *Argo* heard him and longed to be away and rushed into the whispering sea."

Grace and Joel sighed happily. Lottie said, "Then what happened?"

"Then the crew fitted out the *Argo* with food and water and everything they would need, and they rowed away with their oars keeping time to the music of Orpheus's harp."

Lottie frowned. "Is that the end?"

"The end of one story, but there are more after it."

Lottie ducked her head and mumbled something.

"What?"

86

"I said if you stay here with us you can tell one every day till a boat comes for us."

"What if there's more days than stories?" asked Jack.

"I'm sure there aren't," Vinnie said rashly. "Anyway, you can all take turns telling stories to help the time go by."

"And when the boat comes," said Joel, "it will be the *Argo*, and there will be music."

Vinnie stood up. It was beginning to grow dark. The mountains on either side of the village looked like the shoulders of a giant, hunched, settling down to sleep. Lottie pointed up the path. "Who's that?" she asked. It was Andrew with the two boys who had been sent off earlier.

Vinnie led her group of children back to the street to meet Andrew, but before the boys had come down from the path, Nell broke away from the rest. Vinnie stepped after the running child, not to stop her, but just to see what Nell was about. She tore right past the two village boys and, with a strangled cry, hurled herself at Andrew.

He stopped, dumbfounded. Nell flung her arms around his knees. He bent down. He seemed to be speaking to her, because her face, buried against his trousers, tipped up to him. And then she went still. Her arms still locked about him, she neither spoke nor moved.

Vinnie went up to them. She spoke softly. "It's Nell. She thinks she knows you."

Nell stared up at him out of a face turned to stone.

"You're someone to her," Vinnie went on, her voice still low.

Andrew licked his lips. He didn't stir.

Vinnie knelt down beside Nell. "Your brother, Nell?" The child didn't even blink. "Someone from home?"

Nell drew in her breath so sharply, it cut to Vinnie's heart. "Oh, tell me," she whispered. "Please tell me, Nell."

The child's arms fell away, releasing Andrew, who squatted down too. Tears coursed down her grimy cheeks. He said, "I'll be your brother if you like. I'm Andrew, but you can call me . . . his name."

Nell rubbed her dripping nose with her bunched sleeve. She backed three steps, turned, and trudged down to Sue-Lou.

After a moment Andrew and Vinnie started down together. Nell was walking away now, Sue-Lou trailing after her. The two young children turned in to a cottage where the clacking of a loom went on without missing a beat.

"She won't tell us, not ever," Vinnie said. "Something must have happened to her. Maybe only Miss Covington knew."

"We can try to find out," Andrew told her. "We have time."

"You will, maybe, but I'll be back with Peg—"

"No, Vinnie. You're staying here. Didn't you know that?"

At first she didn't believe him. But when he assured her that he was here to learn more weaving and that she and Peg would stay on in the cottage of the parents of Peg's dead husband, he made it sound so straightforward and arranged that she was convinced. That meant she could plan a service for Willie. Maybe Andrew could lead it. She asked him.

"No."

"All you have to do is say a prayer."

"Vinnie, I can't."

"Someone has to. We don't have anyone to do it for us. For Willie, I mean."

"What about Perry?"

"Master Perry. Yes. I suppose." But she dreaded asking him.

She left the rattle and pounding of the looms behind and felt her way along the path. The church loomed dark and squat, and somehow chilling, with its fringe of gravestones lagging to the rear. A dim light glowed through the manse window. It was the first window she had seen in many, many weeks. She stood at the door, her heart pounding, trying to gather the right words to put to him.

"Oh," said Perry when he saw who it was.

She held herself very straight. "I've come about the service for Willie who died. One of our children."

"One of whose?"

"One of us." Why did she feel nervous in front of Master Perry? He was only a boy, not much older than she was. "Willie was buried here."

"So? What do you want of me?"

"To say a prayer. A service at the grave. You're the oldest."

To her immense relief, Perry nodded. He said, "Can you clean the children up?"

She said, "I'll do my best. Do you know the prayer for the dead? The one the captain read?"

He nodded. "I think so. Yes."

"Would tomorrow be all right?"

"Tomorrow? Let me see. I have such a full schedule—"

"Master Perry!"

He gave an exasperated sigh. "All right. Tomorrow."

She turned to go.

"Vinnie?"

She stopped.

"What about a hymn? It would make more of a service."

She thought a moment. "Do they sing hymns at burial services?"

Perry said, "It would sound . . . nice."

It struck her then how alone he was, perhaps the most alone of them all. Except Nell. "Would 'Awake, My Soul' be all right? I think they could sing that if we practice first."

"Yes," he said. "That would be fine." He nodded to her, an almost civil gesture, sending her out into the darkness.

Stumbling until she found the path, she sang under her breath, " 'Awake, my soul, stretch every nerve, and press with vigor on; a heavenly race demands thy zeal, and an immortal crown, and an immortal crown.' " Oh, it was a fine hymn, even if it wasn't exactly a funeral one. It might lift their spirits for a while.

nine ❧

"It's raining!"

Vinnie rolled over and looked up at Lottie. "It's always raining." She gazed around the strange room, all the more strange for being exactly like Peg's cottage at the other end of the island. To her everlasting relief, Peg's father-in-law was too bound up with rheumatism to weave, for others had kept at their looms most of the night.

"When do you have to go back?" Lottie wanted to know.

"Not till spring. Lambing time. I don't even know what month this is. Haven't you had Christmas yet?"

"It might have been the time in church. Vinnie, I found out why the sheep can't stay here. It's because the people dig all the turf around the village for their fires, so there's not enough grazing here for the sheep. Don't you think that's stupid?"

"I don't know," she said, yawning and getting up. She followed her cousin to the door and looked out onto a dreary, wet street. At least, thought Vinnie, the rain spattering on the flagstones muffles the racket of the looms. But Grace and Joel and the others were inside where they couldn't escape the terrible noise. Maybe if they all went down to the manse they could practice the hymn there, out of the rain and away from the looms.

90

She sent Lottie out to fetch them. The village children came too, and it was a sizable group that presented itself at Perry's door —sizable and wet.

"Make them stay over there till they stop dripping," he told Vinnie. "And get that dog out."

Reluctantly Vinnie called Kep to the door.

"So," said Perry, casting his eyes over the steaming knot of children, "which of them is which?"

They all looked back at him. No one spoke up.

"How many of them know the hymn?"

She pointed to Lottie. "And Grace and Joel have sung it but probably don't remember it very well."

"Neither do I," said Lottie. "Only the beginning."

"Call me when they've learned the first verse." Perry turned on his heel and closed himself into the other room.

Joel sidled over to the outside door. Vinnie thought he was about to desert, but it was only to let Kep in again.

She had the children sit down. There was Kep now, his chin on the floor between Joel and Grace. "All right," she began, "Lottie and I will teach you the first words." But after the opening phrase, Vinnie sang alone. She was aware of the intensity of the children's listening. No one stirred. The village children stared with expressions of amazement.

Line by line, repeating the words and music over and over, she dragged the children's voices out. Every time another child seemed to catch on and join in, Jack or Amy or Mabelle, she smiled her encouragement. Finally Grace's friend took part too. She didn't try to pronounce any words, but every time they came to the end of a phrase, Vinnie could hear the new voice along with Joel's comic drone.

Eventually Perry opened the door, listened for a while, and then joined in. His true, deep singing added substance and solemnity. It gave Vinnie courage to sing more fully herself. What did it matter if they didn't have all the words and if the vil-

91

lage children had no words at all? They were a real choir now.

"Second verse," Perry commanded.

" 'A cloud of witnesses around—' " sang Vinnie, but the children's voices fell away. She turned doubtfully to Perry. "Maybe one verse is enough."

Lottie burst out laughing. "You don't even know what they're singing."

"Let's hear it then," Perry answered.

The children shuffled their feet on the puddled floor, their eyes shifting anxiously from Perry to Vinnie. " 'Awake, my soul,' " they sang, subdued, spiritless, " 'stretch every nerve. . . .' "

" 'And press with vigor on,' " Vinnie led the singing.

Lottie was giggling. Master Perry started to laugh too. "Did you hear that? 'A dress with vinegar on'!"

" 'A heavenly race demands thy zeal,' " Vinnie all but bellowed, " 'and an immortal crown. . . .' "

But the children were already beginning to whisper. Everything was ruined.

Perry turned to Grace. "What comes next," he asked, still shaking with laughter.

In a small, self-conscious voice, she sang, " 'An' many more till ground.' " Perry hooted. Grace, close to tears, looked at Vinnie. "Did I get it wrong?"

"There are some wrong words, that's all. They can be fixed."

"But you're cross," Grace whispered.

"Not with you, Grace. Truly not."

"Seems to me," said Perry, "you've quite a bit of fixing to do."

Hugging Grace, Vinnie looked up at him. "Not now," she replied, her voice low. It was hard to keep her anger from rushing into it. "There's nothing to work with now."

Perry shrugged. "It's you who wanted the service."

Jack said, "Aren't we going to? We all learned hard as we could."

92

Laughing again, Perry said, "You're not going to disappoint the lad, are you? If he's happy with the singing—"

"It's not just for him," Vinnie retorted. "It's for everyone."

"*Everyone* can't understand the words, right or wrong, so it can't matter."

"It does matter," Vinnie cried. "It does!"

"Why?" he demanded.

"Because it's a show," Lottie declared. "Vinnie isn't even thinking about Willie anymore."

Stung, Vinnie couldn't speak. Everything was turned around and ugly. Some of the children began to leave. She called to them, "Don't go," but her voice came out harsh and raw. The children trooped off into the rain. Only Grace and Joel and Jack stayed with her to study the proper words. Vinnie's throat ached with the effort to rally them, and the ache went all through her like a fever spreading and taking hold of her.

Maybe it was the hymn that tripped her up like that. Would she never learn to hold back? She could just as well have been at the Stotts again with Perry home from school and the cousins visiting. The cousins wanted Vinnie in their theatrical; someone had to be Cleopatra's maids, and they hadn't nearly enough actors for all the parts. Miss Daisy, the oldest, was Cleopatra. Oh, the terrifying grandeur of that scene with Miss Daisy declaiming to Vinnie: "Give me my robe, put on my crown, I have immortal longings in me." Vinnie could not break out of its spell. Even carrying up the children's bathwater and coal for the nursery fire, she remained the handmaiden of the doomed queen.

She was the handmaiden straight through Sunday worship, when they sang "Awake, My Soul." Later, the teacloth she whipped out for the nursery table became Cleopatra's royal robe. "Give me my robe," Vinnie sang with all the regal splendor at her command. To the melody of "Awake, My Soul," she draped the cloth around her own shoulders: "Put on my crown, I have immortal longings in me." She was so caught up in the drama that she heard neither footsteps nor voices. Only the squeaky door brought her to herself as the cousins and Perry burst in on her. Even as she shed her robe and queenly air, she noticed Perry's sharp eye gleaming dislike. Had he guessed what she was about? Smoothing the cloth on the table, she hummed softly and prayed that her flaming cheeks would not give her away.

Lottie was right about the hymn. Vinnie knew that once again the singing, the spectacle, had pushed out every other thought. She didn't know how you guarded against a nature so readily stirred. For now, all she could do was send the children along with thanks, and then set her mind to practical matters, like getting Andrew to explain to the islanders what she and Perry and the children were about to do. She hoped there would be no objection to entering the graveyard.

In the cottage where Andrew was weaving, a man stood at his shoulder nodding and gesturing like a conductor. The man tapped Andrew and pointed to Vinnie, then took Andrew's place at the loom.

She wanted to be sure it was all right, she explained to Andrew. She wanted him to tell Peg. "Everything," she insisted, when Andrew drew Peg aside to speak with her. "Don't leave out about us being grateful."

Peg's hand came up, the palm pressed against Vinnie's lips.

"You're as bad as the looms," Andrew said. "Clattering on and on." He spoke with Peg awhile, and then turned to Vinnie again. "It's all right. Peg just needs to tell a few people."

Vinnie gathered up the children and led them out of the street, away from the looms. Several of the village children came along with them. They were like Peg's sheep, wary at first, trusting when there was need for trust, but afterward wild again, remote.

The downpour had wrung itself out, and there were only fitful showers now and mist. The children had shed some of their wet outerwear. Master Perry wouldn't approve of the soiled waistcoats and dresses, but he could hardly send the children away. This was their home, not his. What mattered to Vinnie was that they were there. A cloud of witnesses, just as the hymn said. These dirty, lumpy children, who neither belonged with Vinnie's group nor could keep apart, were witnesses enough. Besides, standing among them were Nell and Sue-Lou and the little boys.

" 'A cloud of witnesses around,' " Vinnie started to sing. Jack and the twins and Lottie joined in, but with the words to the first verse instead.

" 'A heavenly race,' " Vinnie sang with them, " 'demands thy zeal. . . .' "

Ahead she saw Perry going around the church to the graveyard to open the gate. They moved toward him as they sang, " 'And an immortal crown.' " Or at least some of them sang that.

The wall glistened, dark and clean. Inside the graveyard the sodden weeds, already winter-killed, stood broken but tall.

" 'Awake, my soul,' " she started all over, and the children, some using the proper hymn phrases, some a language of their own hearing, and others no words at all, threw themselves into the singing as they bunched together.

Joel slipped his hand in Vinnie's. "Look. Behind us."

Still singing, Vinnie turned. The path was full of people, the old and bent, the straight and lean, the heavy and slow. No one hurried. They moved like melting snow shifting down the slope. On they came, women with white fringes over their foreheads and shawls covering their hair, men in homespun jackets over their shirts and waistcoats.

There was no writing on any of the gravestones, nothing to set one burial place apart from another. It was simply that some stones were large, some small, some tiny. Willie's was small. Perry stood behind it while the children gathered, Jack in front of Vinnie, leaning ever so lightly against her. The islanders drew up in silence all around the children.

After a long pause, Perry asked in an undertone, "What is Willie's full name?"

Vinnie thought. "Durston?" She set her hands on Jack's shoulders.

"And the other one? The missing boy?"

"Toby? Oh, no, Toby's not dead."

"The prayer can be for two as well as one," Perry offered.

"Just start," she hissed. "This is for Willie, who is here."

Perry spoke the name and then, with schoolboy speed, raced through the prayer for the dead. Vinnie's heart sank. You couldn't catch the words that way, couldn't feel them. She drew a long breath. She would have to begin the hymn.

But someone behind her spoke out from among the islanders. "'The Lord is my shepherd; I shall not want. . . .'" It was Andrew's voice, but with a difference. He must have learned the psalm from his mother or his grandfather, for he recited with a lilt that she hadn't heard in him before. When he came to "The valley of the shadow of death," she could feel Jack straighten and pull away; she let him go.

After the psalm was finished, she waited for the last words to settle before beginning to sing. The children trailed after her, a ragged start. Then they picked up as they moved on; it was all right, for they were all witnesses now, singers and watchers alike.

It was only later as the people nearest the gate turned to go, that she caught sight of Perry, his mouth set grimly, following Andrew with his eyes. Vinnie and her little ones were the last to leave. She saw Peg waiting beyond the gate, and sent the children on. They broke into a run, even Jack shedding his gravity to speed off with them down toward the beach.

Perry strode back to her. "Did you arrange that surprise?"

"You mean the psalm? No, I didn't think of it. I'm glad we had it, though."

"Next time, then, get *him* to run your service."

"That's a terrible thing to say. There isn't going to be a next time." How could they stand there quarreling like this after praying and singing for Willie?

96

Perry swung past her and left. She could hear the children's voices down the path. She turned to follow Peg, who stepped carefully around the stones and made her way to the far upland edge of the graveyard. Here stood one great stone facing nine tiny ones in rows of three. Peg swept her hand from one to another like a hen winging over its chicks. Then her shawl closed around her. She wrapped herself tight, all gray but for the fringe of white at her brow, like a grave slab.

Vinnie looked from Peg to the stones, three rows of three, nine babies dead. Peg had carried and given birth to nine children, and every one was buried here.

Standing behind Peg, Vinnie moved closer until she was leaning as Jack had done. She reached her arm around Peg's arm and with it pressed the body that stood like a granite slab but was not stone, was flesh and blood and bone and heart. Vinnie could feel the pulse throbbing from her hand to Peg's.

Down toward the beach the children's voices died away. There was an instant when nothing stirred and the dim light sealed itself into a fraction of eternity. Then the light opened out and shadows appeared, one for every upright stone among the weeds. At that moment the village looms split the silence. The din spilled out onto the street and down the path and into the churchyard and up to where the mountains rose and fell again toward the sea.

Beyond the human and inhuman clamor, the sea hurled itself in its mighty greed and was shattered and made whole all over again, gathering life from death, ceaseless and famished.

ten 🦢

Every morning the men gathered on the street. Sometimes they examined ropes or looked over a part from a broken loom. Sometimes they just talked. As soon as they returned to their looms, the women came out. Some of them knitted, some spun. They talked too, with the village children running among them, usually bringing smiles and touches as they passed by. But during the men's time on the street, the children kept out of the way.

Andrew, neither child nor man, was seldom out and never long enough to spend any time with Vinnie, until a day came when a loom was carried out of a cottage and its door was shut. It was the first time Vinnie had seen a cottage door closed.

"The baby will be born soon." Andrew spoke behind her. "Everything will be different for a while."

Vinnie was sent with the children to the shore to carry up driftwood. By the time she came back, Andrew and the two village boys were leaning against the cottage walls like the men. The looms were all silent, the wind rising, the village dogs tucking in their tails and curling against the coming of rough weather.

As soon as Andrew caught Vinnie's eye, he beckoned her and slowly moved off. Vinnie went ahead, climbing over the kale yard walls and continuing on uphill. Kep bounded over to her, full of glee because his master had come outside with him again. Then Andrew reappeared, running too, reminding Vinnie of those first times at the other end of the island.

Passing Vinnie, Andrew charged on. He leaped over outcroppings and sailed over clumps of heather. On he went, Vinnie clambering after him. He didn't stop until he had scaled the rocky heights. Then they stood side by side, the wind whipping tears from their eyes as they looked down the far slope where once Vinnie had hoped she might find adults in a solitary cottage like Peg's. But there were no cottages, only a few more cleits, round and squat on the bare hill that fell away to the sea.

Surely this was the end of the world. It was hard to believe in anything beyond. Buffalo in America? Halifax in Canada? What if all they ever knew of those places was what they could dream? Think of remaining here year after year, with the wind and the ocean beating this tiny land with salt spray, flinging seaweed so high you could stoop here on this ridge and pick up a perfect shell.

"Are they finished weaving?" she asked.

He shook his head. "They're worried, because they fell behind schedule when they were sick. And now there's the baby. They'll have to stop for the mourning."

"Mourning! Andrew, how can you say that?"

He just looked at her and started down the hill. Vinnie pulled her shawl around her face and leaned into the wind. They were coming to the cluster of cleits. Here at last there would be some shelter. But Andrew kept going, past the first cleit and the second and third. At the fourth one, he ducked in through the low door Vinnie was close behind.

They wiped their eyes and noses, then sank to the earthen floor. The wall curved inward, but they leaned against it anyway. Vinnie's legs were trembling.

"Hold Kep," Andrew said. "He'll warm you."

Kep squirmed at first; then he nestled close. Vinnie could feel her fingers now, her face. As she grew used to the darkness, she began to notice stacks of things that weren't dried birds. Rising to her knees, she peered at something that looked like a box, a travel box, and beside it some lumpy sacking. She raised a corner of the cloth and saw beneath it a child's cloak. Here was another, and another. Over there, where she next groped, were shifts and aprons and bodices. There were shoes and a wooden cane. She returned to the travel box and tried to pry it open.

"You have to unfasten the straps," Andrew told her.

She rocked back on her heels. So he already knew about it! He had brought her here to show her.

Andrew reached past her and picked up something that he draped across his arms. "My jacket. Too small now. But I have found another, here, and trousers as well, and when the time comes I intend to wear them."

"Oh, Andrew."

"There's money in the box," he told her. "And a book and candlesticks and gloves and bonnets." He pulled the strap free and raised the lid. "And, oh yes, I forgot." Out came a black hat. He set it on his head. "Do I look a gentleman?" He took it off and knocked brine or mold from it.

Everything smelled of mildew, but Vinnie couldn't stop rummaging. Piece after piece was taken to the doorway to be examined. The book was only a ledger, and anyway the pages were all stuck together. Then Andrew drew out something with real printed words—part of a magazine.

" 'Preparing for Sunday!' " she read. It was the *Infant's Magazine* she had shoved inside Nell's bodice to protect her from the wind. It must have stayed inside Nell's clothes until they were taken off.

Vinnie tried to turn the pages, but like the ledger they were glued together. So she read aloud what she could:

100

Haste! Put your playthings all away,
Tomorrow is the Sabbath-day
Come! Bring me your Noah's ark,
Your pretty, tinkling music-cart
Because, my love, you must not play,
But holy keep the Sabbath-day.

She turned to Andrew. "Won't Grace and Joel be glad! Just think, if we can get these pages apart, we'll have songs and stories—"

"No!" His voice was cutting. "You mustn't let anyone know you've seen these things."

She stared at him, astonished, bewildered. "I can't take anything? Not even my own apron?" She could feel hot tears on her cold cheeks. "Only what belongs to us," she whispered. "Why not?"

"Because," he said in a low voice, "if they find out you know what's here, they will hide these things again, and next time we may not find them."

"But, Andrew, they're not hidden. They're only put away for us."

"Covered with sackcloth? Kept so far from us? Vinnie, here's proof that everything I've said is true. Perhaps the islanders mean to use or trade them sometime; they certainly don't intend us to have them. You just don't want to admit that."

She was shaking her head and crying. She couldn't stop. Kep dove in under her arms and licked her face. Andrew put an arm around her shoulders and waited.

Finally she asked, "Are there . . . other books?" She was thinking of *The Heroes.* If she had just that one possession, she would be fine.

"I don't know. I don't think we should stay too long now. But if you pick a time like today when they're all fixed on something else, maybe you can get back again and look." He started putting everything back, but then he stopped to show her one other object. "Look. I think it's fur. Isn't it soft?"

He handed the thing to Vinnie. The fur was both soft and matted. "A muff," she whispered. "A fur muff." She was a little girl again.

"That would be handy to have."

But Vinnie scarcely heard him. "I had a little fur muff once," she murmured. "Someone gave it me."

Andrew laughed. "I suppose you wore it to work making matchboxes."

Vinnie flushed. What had made her say that? She pulled her shawl up over her head. "Did you show me these things just to convince me?" she asked him.

"Not just that," he said. "But in case I'm away when a ship comes. I've been thinking about it a lot while I've been at the loom. I know you think I've made it all up. But if I'm right, Vinnie, you'll need to get the clothes for the little children. Don't worry about Lottie or Jack. Even Grace can speak for herself. See to the ones who can't or won't speak."

They stayed a moment longer, Vinnie wondering whether these things were stolen or simply salvaged, and not quite sure what the difference was.

Andrew said, "My grandfather once found an ancient flint, an elf-shot, he called it. He gave it to my brother. I wanted it so. When I held it in my hand, I felt it was mine. I thought and thought of stealing it."

"What happened?"

"Nothing. My brother lost it. I was sure I must have taken that flint and that was why he couldn't find it. I gave him a marble and a feather and a silver key, all my treasures."

Vinnie couldn't help smiling. "What I told you just now, that I'd had a muff, probably that was from wanting one when I was little. Sometimes I misremember. I think things or see things I'm sure are truc that can't be."

102

"It's strange how notions just come to you when you least expect them. Like that about the elf-shot."

"I know. Once my granny took me sliding on the ice and—" She broke off. She clapped her hand to her mouth.

"Go on," urged Andrew.

"No, I'm wrong. I'm doing it again, making something up." She shook her head. She could feel her fingers growing cold. That false memory stuck, and with it came the face she used to see in her dreams sometimes and in the Stotts' mirror. Not just a face either, but a whole person, thick and lumbering like a bear. Like a bear too in playfulness, swinging Vinnie onto the ice, then tumbling, both of them, laughing. And the sky was a broken looking glass, fragments of blue between black cracks . . . black, bare twisted branches . . . Granny somewhere between, staggering and laughing, her bonnet askew, its ribbons fluttering across Vinnie's face. Granny was a dancing bear in a black bonnet, her great paw mopping the snow from Vinnie's face. Vinnie reached for the hand, missed and grasped instead at the black ribbons that bounced away and away into the dazzling light, into the mirror all crazed with jagged cracks, and the face cracked and lined and laughing, laughing . . .

". . . imagining about your granny?" Andrew was asking.

Vinnie nodded. "I suppose I'm confusing her with Peg on the ice." Her voice dropped. "I don't think I ever saw my granny."

They went out into the bitter wind. But for Vinnie, the images refused to disperse or fade, and the cold assaulted her from within as much as from outside. If her memory could play her false like this, what must it be like for the little ones? No wonder some of them forgot who they were. They should be having lessons and prayers and songs. They mustn't be allowed to slip into the island rhythm.

She thought briefly, longingly, about the *Infant's Magazine* left in the box in the cleit. If she read that rhyme to Nell, what sense could the child make of a Noah's ark or a music-cart?

Vinnie hugged her shawl about her and scrambled to catch up with Andrew, even though she knew they would have to part before they reached the village.

That afternoon, to Vinnie's surprise, Perry agreed to her giving the children regular lessons in the manse.

"But what can you do without slates or pencils or books?" he wanted to know.

She thought of the things hidden in the cleit. But she had no right to give away the secret Andrew had shared with her. "Isn't there a Bible, an English one? They could memorize a few verses every day."

"They could have arithmetic lessons too, and natural science." He rubbed his hands. They looked blotchy, the knuckles swollen. He was still wearing his threadbare clothes, still apart from everyone else.

On an impulse she asked him if he would help, since he knew more about those kinds of studies. At first he seemed almost eager, but then he said, "Of course we'll divide up. I'll teach my children, you teach yours."

"Mine?"

"Miss Covington's then. You know very well what I mean."

"Master Perry," she said, trying to keep her voice level, "the division should be either by subject or by age. And as for Joel and Grace, your mother trusted me to teach them some of what she taught me."

"I know that." Perry's mottled fingers clenched. "For weren't you always there at my table when I came home. As if you belonged."

"I never meant to take your place. I never tried to."

"Well, you didn't know your own place, did you?"

Vinnie swallowed her next retort. Her project was falling to ruins before it had even begun. She didn't know how to deal with him. It seemed to mean nothing to him that Willie was dead and that they had lost Toby and had no idea what had become of the rest of Miss Covington's charges. "I don't even know their names," she said.

"Whose?"

"The other children in steerage. Come to that, I don't really know Sue-Lou's name or the little boys'."

"What little boys?"

"Two boys from another shipwreck. One was a new baby when he was brought here. The other, the one the islanders call Gillie, looks about Joel's age, maybe a little younger. They are so much like the islanders now, you'd never guess they weren't. I don't want that to happen to any of Miss Covington's children."

"All right. All right then. Though I haven't the slightest idea what I'm to do with their sort."

"They're not ignorant," Vinnie reminded him. "It's true some are out of Ragged Schools or workhouses, but others must come from homes like Lottie's. She was taken by Miss Covington because my aunt went into service and couldn't keep a child. Anyway, all the children have been prepared. If you give them a chance, Master Perry, I think you'll find that your mother's scheme was working."

"We'll see," he said. Vinnie took it as a grudging consent.

She wanted to prove to him straight off that the older children would be worthy of his tutoring, but the village excitement over the birth of a baby boy postponed the first lesson.

The street was like a hive. Women passed in and out of the cottage where the mother and her new son lay, the door always closing behind. The men picked over the stack of driftwood and started to build a cradle for the baby. The children played a game with wood chips and sticks, charging up and down the street, even dashing against the men when they couldn't dodge around them.

At one point Vinnie found herself beside Andrew. "There," she remarked, "you were wrong. Everyone's celebrating."

105

Andrew shook his head. "It always starts like this. You'll see."

Jack charged into them, the twins in pursuit. Mabelle swung wide and stumbled against the unfinished cradle. She thrust out her hand to keep from falling.

Jack brought her to Vinnie. There was a spot of blood on the heel of Mabelle's palm.

"It's nothing," Vinnie said. "It's hardly bleeding. Just be more careful."

Mabelle ran off with Amy and Jack.

But later her mama fussed over the tiny wound, and Mabelle was taken into the cottage where the new baby lived. When she came out, she had a bit of sacking wrapped around her hand. She came shouting to Vinnie, "I have seen the baby. I'm the only one allowed, because I hurt myself."

Grace pushed past her. "Oh, please may I go in? Look, I have a scratch too." Grace thrust forward a finger. "I need a bandage, don't I?"

"And medicine too," Mabelle told her. "It stopped the hurt. It's special medicine for the baby and me."

"Listen," Vinnie announced, "we are going to have school. You are going to be kept busy with lessons."

"But Mabelle saw the baby—"

"Go and bring Lottie and Jack and Joel and Nell. And Sue-Lou. We'll have a little talk with Master Perry and decide who will be with the scholars and who with the infants."

She guided them firmly down the path to the manse, her mind racing ahead of her, trying to settle on some scheme that would put the children in the best light.

They clustered around the stove, holding up raw hands and thrusting back their jackets and shawls to let the warmth in under the thick homespun. Vinnie tried to see them as Perry must. They looked a little wary, but ready to burst into play or song or whatever task she might set them to. Could Perry sense their willingness, their brightness, or did he see only the unshorn heads and the dirt and the ill-fitting, primitive clothing?

Out of nowhere her mother's ritual for lessons came to her. She said, "What is the world?"

The children all looked at her, waiting for a clue.

"What is the world?" she repeated.

Lottie scowled. She opened her mouth, then shut it again.

"What is the world?" Vinnie said for the third time.

"The earth . . ." Lottie replied. She swallowed, her gaze fixed on Vinnie. "The earth we dwell on," she declared more firmly.

"Who made it?"

"God. No, no. The great and good God."

Vinnie could feel the listening all about her, all of them, even and especially Perry. She beamed at Lottie and asked, "Are there not many things in it you would like to know about?"

"Yes," Lottie answered. "Yes, yes, yes." And she burst into tears.

Vinnie gave Lottie a hug and then quickly excused her before her outburst unsettled the others. The children were all keyed up, she explained to Perry; the whole village was. She was sure things would quiet down in a day or so. And then the lessons could begin.

A few days later the quiet came, and it was more than she had bargained for. Almost every ordinary activity was suspended. Men and women alike clustered. Restless, they wandered back and forth across the street, like shuttles on the warp of a loom. The cloth they wove with their coming and going was dense with sombre threads pulled so tight they seemed about to break.

A thin, watery sunlight turned the usual puddles into mirrors and the people into shadows. On this day the door was opened and the baby carried into the street for all to see. He snuffled and mewed like a kitten, and all the shadows tilted toward him.

Mabelle said he had already grown. How could she tell? Vinnie

107

wondered. Yet she took Mabelle's remark as a sign that all was well.

After the baby was taken back inside, Vinnie called the children for school. They passed the cradle, still in the street, still wanting its rockers, and started down the path. Grace had her nearly grown friend Thora in tow, even though Vinnie pointed out that Thora wouldn't be able to understand the lesson.

"She wants to come with us, though," Grace responded. "She can take Lottie's place."

"Lottie will take her own place. Why do you say that?"

"Because Lottie doesn't want lessons. She cried when she recited."

"That's not why she cried."

All the children crowded around, interested.

"Lottie cried," Vinnie told Grace and the others, "because she misses her . . . home so very much."

"So do I," Grace promptly replied. "I miss my mother and father."

Joel tugged at Vinnie's shawl. "Do you know my father, Vinnie?"

"Yes, Joel."

"So do I." He kicked at a pebble. "Only I can't see him." His face was all screwed up. "Sometimes I think I see Mother, though."

"That's because your father went away to Canada before we did. It's been a long time without him. When you get there and see him again, you'll remember him perfectly well."

"Then," said Joel, "I won't need to remember." He grinned up at her. "Because he'll be there. He'll talk to me."

Grace said, "I don't think Nell remembers anything."

Vinnie thought maybe it was the other way around. Maybe Nell couldn't bear to think about what she remembered. Vinnie couldn't say that, though, not to Grace. "Soon it will be spring," she told her, "and then the sky will clear and the ocean will settle and a boat will come and take you to your mother."

They walked on. Vinnie felt Lottie's hand slip into her free one. Lottie spoke in an undertone. "I didn't know I could say that. About the world and God. I didn't know I remembered. It just came, the way your mama used to make us say it."

Vinnie nodded. She couldn't comfort Lottie with the words she had spoken to Grace. Lottie had been sent away from her mother, sent for her own sake to a better life.

They were already seated on the floor in the school room when Perry came in from his private room. His first glance took in several newcomers. "Send them away," he ordered.

Vinnie, spreading shawls and mufflers to dry, looked up to find him standing with his arms folded across his chest. "I cannot," she told him. "They are the children of our hosts."

He let his eyes flicker over the group of waiting children, then pointed with the toe of his shoe. "Look at that. An infant."

"One of ours."

"That little fellow?" Perry sounded truly taken aback. "The little one with the cap?"

Vinnie nodded. "One of those I was telling you about. He may be too young to understand, but he needs to hear us."

"And the girls with him?"

"Islanders. As far as we know."

"What do you mean by that?"

"There are children here from at least one earlier shipwreck. Master Perry, will you begin with a psalm this morning?"

He read, " 'I will lift up mine eyes unto the hills.' " When that was finished, she took the youngest children to the other end of the room while the older ones stayed with Perry to learn the psalm.

Vinnie told her group to pretend there were hills to look up to and to imagine catching sight of something wonderful there.

109

Grace flung back her head. Joel copied his sister, and then the twins followed. Soon even the village children were gazing at the ceiling.

Vinnie praised them all. "Now," she said, "remember the words in the psalm: 'I will lift up mine eyes unto the hills, from whence cometh my help. . . .' You are looking at the hills. What do you see?"

"I see something shiny," Joel declared in his growly voice.

"Good. It's radiant. Is it a star?"

"I think," said Joel, "it's a crack in the roof."

"She wants you to say star," said Grace, "like the star of Bethlehem."

Joel shook his head. "I don't think it's that. Anyway, they don't have stars in the daytime."

One of the twins whimpered and dropped her head forward. "Try to keep your head back," Vinnie said. And then she told Joel, "It's like seeing your mother even though she's not right here. Only now, instead of someone you know and love, you are to imagine some sign, something godlike."

"Mabelle isn't lifting her eyes unto the hills," Grace told Vinnie.

"Can you see anything?" Vinnie pressed Joel.

"Books," he said. "I see books and books and books."

"That's Father's study," Grace informed him. "Do you remember that?"

He shook his head.

"But you do," she insisted. "That's what you're seeing. Otherwise how do you know they are books?"

"My neck hurts," Mabelle whispered. "Please, miss, can I go?"

"Mabelle always has something the matter with her," Grace complained. "Last time she got to see the baby."

"Mabelle, we're going to do sums next. And then geography."

But the lesson wasn't working. The village children were a distraction. Thora refused to stay with the older group, and ended

110

up rocking Mabelle on her lap. Vinnie told Grace to ask Thora to take Mabelle back to the village, but by then the energy and purpose had gone out of Vinnie. The recitation across the room jarred her nerves. She couldn't hold the children's attention.

Tomorrow, Vinnie thought. Tomorrow Mabelle would feel better, and they would settle into the new routine with the village children among them. Tomorrow they would make up for the disorder of today.

eleven 🦎

Overnight the weather changed. It made Vinnie want to race down the steep slope. The children skipped and darted like fish in shallows. Even Mabelle couldn't resist the lightness in the air. She ran after the other children to collect seaware washed up on the rocks.

"How long will they be at the seaweed?" Vinnie asked Andrew.

Until the tide rose, he guessed. Several hours probably. The islanders would take advantage of this warm spell while it lasted. The false spring, his mother used to call it, but his granddad always spoke of it as the cuckoo's greening.

"Well," said Vinnie, "I should tell Master Perry they're not coming for a while."

Andrew said nothing.

"He does care," she added.

Still Andrew didn't answer.

"I think he's changing. Just think, he's giving lessons to children he wouldn't have spoken to before."

Andrew snorted. "He'll always have to be better than everyone else. He doesn't understand that here we're all the same."

Vinnie smiled. "I'm not sure the islanders think so. If you stayed with them, I expect they'd make you their king."

112

"Well, I wouldn't want to be anyone's king." He looked out over the bay, his eyes on the far horizon. "I want to be an apprentice printer in Buffalo in the United States of America. That's what I want." He turned to Vinnie. "What do you intend to be?"

She couldn't very well say: a princess, a queen. "I haven't thought much about it," she confessed. Then, to be truthful, she said, "When I was little, my mama told such stories. They grew into my dreams."

"But you must have some idea," he insisted.

"Not a turnip digger."

"Nor a nursemaid, I should think. You can do better than that."

"Like what?"

"A governess? Or maybe a teacher, but in a school with real scholars and a living. How would that be?"

She blushed to think that the only future she had ever considered came out of fairy tales, with a messenger riding up to her door, trumpets blaring, a proclamation restoring her to her lost realm. "I haven't thought much beyond the next few years with the Stotts."

"You plan to go back to England with them after their time in Canada?"

"I suppose so."

Andrew was shocked. "When all the real opportunity is in America?"

"I don't know." How had the conversation taken this turn? Vinnie's thoughts were all tangled; they had no beginnings, no ends.

While they had been talking, a large cluster of villagers formed, sprang apart, and regrouped. Voices rose. There was a flurry of activity near the cottage with the mother and baby, a stridency.

"What is it?" Vinnie whispered. "What are they saying?"

Andrew shook his head. "I can't tell. They're all talking at once."

In a little while the excitement subsided. The silent waiting resumed. So it was nothing important, Vinnie told herself. Everything was all right.

But on her way to the manse she saw that the unfinished cradle had been moved to the middle of the street. They were going to put the rockers under it, she thought. At last.

Thora met her and tugged at her sleeve. She pointed first to the children trudging up the hill with baskets of seaware, then toward the gardens above the village. Vinnie and Thora were to spread the seaware over the ground.

It was pleasant out on the hill. Gulls and fulmars glided overhead, delighting, it seemed, in the warm currents of air. The light on the rolling moorland softened everything it touched. The children returned with more seaware, even the littlest carrying some in slimy red-green bundles.

"Please, miss." Amy stopped before Vinnie. "Mabelle won't come."

Vinnie sighed. Her back was beginning to ache with the constant lifting and lowering of the slippery seaware. "Tell her she must."

"Please, miss, you tell her."

Mabelle was on the path near the manse. She was sitting with her knees up, her chin resting on them.

Irritation swept through Vinnie. "Get right up. Look at this mess." She pointed to the seaware sprawled along the side of the path. "You can't just sit there." When Mabelle made no move to get up, Vinnie's voice rose. "Mabelle, did you hear me?"

Mabelle looked up then. She was making a face. It wasn't exactly defiant or impudent, but it was certainly ugly, with her mouth pulled down in a grimace, her cheeks contorted.

"Stop that!" Vinnie shook her. "Stop it, stop it."

She knew the other children were gathering, yet holding back a little too. She wanted to shut her eyes and clench her fists and scream and scream. "Don't be sick," she shrilled. "Don't you dare be sick."

She felt someone behind her, a hand on her shoulder. She turned. Peg was there, and other women.

"She won't work," Vinnie rasped. "She won't get up. I don't know what to do with her."

Peg bent down to Mabelle and looked into her face. She spoke with the other women. They came together to carry Mabelle to the village. Peg walked Vinnie back, her arm around her.

Vinnie felt hot, too hot. She was scared. She kept trying to explain that it wasn't her fault and that she didn't know what to do. She kept railing at Mabelle for misbehaving, for getting her feet wet, for missing lessons and missing work. She didn't dare stop berating the child. She had to hear her anger in that silent village. She had to go on showing them all, showing herself too, that there was absolutely nothing wrong with that naughty child.

By the next day all the children had somehow learned that the new baby had stopped eating and was beginning to fail. Vinnie tried to make Mabelle more comfortable by washing the sticky residue of seaware from her hands and face, but Mabelle twisted away to avoid the cloth. It hurt, she said between clenched teeth. Vinnie promised to be gentle. Like this, she said, stroking Mabelle's skin as lightly as possible. But Mabelle cried. It hurt, everything hurt. Where? How? Filled with dread, Vinnie craved to know, so she would hurt too.

During the following days there was less and less that Vinnie could do. She took hold of Amy, sometimes telling her stories, sometimes rocking her. She held on to Amy for dear life.

Sometimes Peg came and led Vinnie away. She would only go when Amy was asleep on the sheepskin beside the bed cupboard. On the third or fourth day, Vinnie saw that the cradle in the street had turned into a coffin. She felt nothing at all. Somewhere among the men in the street, Andrew must be standing, but she couldn't see him. Grace and Joel came to hug her as though she had been away for a long time. She asked Lottie if they were all right, and Lottie told her that Thora was looking after them.

"Is Mabelle going to die?" Lottie asked.

"What?" said Vinnie as if it were an outlandish question. Only then she panicked. She had to get back to Mabelle. Firmly, insistently, Peg guided her away. They struggled in silence, until Peg gave in.

Back in the cottage, Mabelle sat right up as if she had never been sick at all. Vinnie shouted with joy and bent down to hug the child. But Mabelle hurled herself back. Her body jerked, it danced and leaped. Her face became a horrible mask with blood and saliva dribbling from the corners of her turned-down mouth.

Peg carried Amy out of the cottage. By the time she returned with Mabelle's mama, Mabelle was lying rigid, her back arched, her fingers spread wide.

Mabelle had two more seizures during the night. Each time, her mama tried to clasp her, to contain the frenzy, but it was too strong. It shook off Mabelle's mama and Peg, and it would have shaken Vinnie as well if she hadn't been too frightened to try holding on.

In between the seizures, Vinnie squeezed a little water into the side of Mabelle's mouth. The child couldn't open it anymore; she couldn't unclench her teeth. Vinnie had to wipe up most of the water. She stroked the pale hair, the contorted face. Mabelle, her eyebrows drawn up, wore a look of surprise, but her eyes held misery, terror.

The wind freshened. Vinnie could hear it moan. The square of light inside the door brought the wild spring air to the hearth and sent dust and ashes flying. Vinnie told Mabelle that the sun was shining and that soon a boat would come and take them home.

The sun was still there when the wind hunched down outside the door and changed its voice. Mabelle's mama and Peg clutched each other. The wind had many voices, all wailing. They sent shivers down Vinnie's back.

Andrew stepped inside. He stood in the block of sunshine and spoke a word or two to Peg, who nodded. He told Vinnie that the baby had died. The islanders would be keening like this for days, not only when burying the baby, but for days and days, wailing with the voices of the wind.

In the afternoon Amy came and stared for a while at the rigid, grotesque figure in the bed cupboard. Then she shook her head as though denying that this was her twin sister. After a few minutes she walked away.

Later she returned, just to check. Vinnie was trying to trickle a little water between Mabelle's clenched teeth. Amy said, "It's too noisy outside."

"Stay here then."

Amy nodded. Yawning, she settled down beside the fire. And while she slept, and while all through the village the people keened for the infant baby boy, Mabelle had her last convulsion. When it was over, she was dead.

Days of wailing followed the burials in the stone-cluttered graveyard. Vinnie held herself aloof from the village mourners. She held herself so tight her body ached. The backs of her legs and her shoulders were as sore as if she had crawled the length of an enormous turnip field, hauling a full sack all the way. Yet she did nothing at all.

Peg attended her, always ready at the first sign of need to draw Vinnie into her arms and hold her quietly. In time, Vinnie learned that she could turn to Peg when the wind and wailing drove her frantic, for there was no escaping them.

Then one morning Vinnie woke to the sound of ordinary voices. Rain spattered the flagstones and dribbled down the chimney hole in the thatch. The embers sizzled. She lay still, soaking in the small, familiar sounds of life.

117

The looms took over once more. They creaked and rattled. The walls throbbed. Again, speakers had to shout above the din.

Vinnie shook out her shawl and drew it over her head. She would go to Amy and the other children. She would take them to the manse.

The mild spell was behind them. The winds were terrific; storm clouds raced across the sky. It was natural for a child to stay inside on a day like this, but Amy had attached herself to her new mama; she had to be pried away.

"She's not your real mama," Vinnie reminded Amy as she pushed her arms into the woolen jumper and wrapped her in a shawl.

In the rain-lashed days that followed, they played Amy's favorite games and sang her favorite songs. Vinnie told Amy's favorite stories so many times that Joel and Grace stopped listening and started quarreling instead.

"Can't you control them?" Perry shouted from across the room, where his group was doing sums. But Vinnie's children stayed crabby—except for Nell, who was simply remote, unreachable.

Coming out of the schoolroom one afternoon, they found the sun again. The world was dazzling, puddles mirroring patches of blue, rocks glistening, the entire rain-drenched slope changing color before their eyes.

"Magic!" breathed Grace.

"Spring," declared Jack.

The sea shivered. Silver-edged clouds rolled past. There were gulls and fulmars everywhere, white flecks swooping and diving under swiftly changing cloud shadows.

Joel called Perry to the door to see this wonder.

Perry clutched his worn, wrinkled coat as he stepped into the wind. "It didn't happen of a sudden," he told Joel. "We just didn't notice it was going on, ever since that warm spell. All these weeks. We didn't notice because of the storms." He ducked back out of the wind.

The children ran shouting up the hill. Thora stopped beside Vinnie and spoke slowly. Something was about to happen, something to look forward to.

"Something good?" Vinnie responded.

"Guid," Thora repeated with a broad smile.

The days that followed brought intermittent rains, but the sun was never gone for long. Amy could be persuaded to play again. Vinnie could relax her vigil; she could work with Nell and Sue-Lou and little Gillie now.

But there was new village work to be done too, nets to mend and baskets to weave, crottle to be scraped from the rocks to make dye for the tweed. She came across sheltered pockets in the hills with wildflowers in bud, but Thora wouldn't let anyone touch them. "Not yet," Grace translated for Vinnie. "She says they are the First Flowers."

One of their forays to collect crottle brought them close to the cleits across the island. Vinnie couldn't get her mind off the magazine and the muff and the ledger book and all the other salvaged things. She thought about going back to see them some early morning. But daily now more men appeared in the street or above the village, turning the soil in the walled plots. She was afraid of being noticed.

Like the hillside greening, the end of the tweed-making caught Vinnie unaware. All at once looms were dismantled and stacked. And Andrew finally emerged, blinking and pale.

Later, when things got back to normal for him, she would speak to him about the cleit. She would convince him that the children needed those reminders, needed to use some of their own belongings.

Thora came running to take Vinnie away. She spoke rapidly, with happiness.

119

"It's time to pick flowers," Andrew told Vinnie. He rubbed his arms and stretched.

"Come with us. You'll like being outdoors."

Andrew shook his head. No men or boys for the First Flowers and the First Egg.

There was laughter and teasing before the girls and younger women set out. The married women, those with white at the front of their headkerchiefs, formed a living basket that scooped up the maidens from the village. "London Bridge," shrieked Grace as Peg tucked her into the midst of the girls.

Once they had passed the plots and fields, the children broke free and raced uphill. The village girls knew exactly where to head; Vinnie's girls pelted after them. They climbed high enough to be able to look out to sea in three directions. Here the grasses swelled in green waves. The children ran through them, plucking whitecaps and yellowcaps.

Vinnie remembered how she had wanted to tear down the slope the day the air changed at the false spring. Now she watched Thora dive like a black seabird as she fished the sward for flowers.

Grace came to Vinnie in tears because Lottie said her stems were too short. She held up a fistful of blue and yellow blooms.

"It doesn't matter. They're lovely."

"It does," Lottie said, just behind her. "There must be stems to string them together."

"Never mind," Vinnie whispered to Grace, "we'll make our own nosegay."

"Even if it's pretty," Lottie flung back, "it'll be wrong."

Vinnie said, "We're not islanders. We don't have to have the same rules." But Lottie was already out of earshot.

After they came back to the village, the women and girls set to work, some in the fields, some to turn and carry the rowing boats to the beach. Vinnie was loaded down with gear to lug to the beach too. Everything was made ready for a visit to the far island. Oats and barley, hidden away until now, were brought to

120

every cottage, and each maiden had a turn grinding the stone three times, always to the right, or sunwise. The children were eager for the bread, for the street was filled with the aroma of baking, but it was all set aside.

The next day was too blustery for the boats. The children stayed close to the cottages, yearning for the bread.

"You'd think," Vinnie remarked to Andrew when he came down from the fields, "they'd let the little ones have some." She could feel her own stomach clench with hunger for it.

"No one eats any until the First Loaf is left with the egg in the earth house. They are for the future, that there may always be corn and always be fowl on those cliffs."

"They go all the way out to the far island just for that? They could get an egg right here. The fulmars have already started nesting."

"But the fulmar lays only one egg, and if it's taken, there will be no young to harvest in the summer. So you see the islanders have reasons for their ways. They will gather some fulmar eggs on the outer islands, and later on some birds. But here on the home island they are far more saving. They'll take the eggs of guillemots and puffins, but they depend on the fulmars here for food and oil, so they will not touch their eggs."

When the wind dropped and the waves subsided, everyone went down to the shore. There was a good deal of confusion while dogs were thrown out of the boats, and baskets were packed around the sitting and kneeling girls and young women. Lottie came along, but Grace and the other smaller girls had to stay behind. With all the village cheering, the boats were pushed off.

Vinnie gripped the gunwale. All she could think of was the *Roger F. Laing* wallowing and sinking. Thora patted her whitened knuckles. She showed Vinnie the strong arms of the rowers, the curving buoyant waves, the mild sky.

When the boats rounded the cliffs near Peg's end of the island, it seemed as though all the seafowl took to wing. The air was shrill with birdcalls. The boats surged forward with every thrust of the oars. The women and girls chattered and laughed. But Vinnie fought nausea and terror. She promised herself that if she ever set foot on dry land again, she would never leave it.

By the time the skillful rowers brought them in among the jagged rocks so the girls and women could leap ashore, Vinnie's numb, white fingers were useless. The others had to take her the way they hoisted the sacks and baskets they cast onto the rocks. They were shouting at her, but the screaming birds were all she could hear. She screamed too, and was yanked and held, soaked and shivering against the cliff.

Someone handed her a basket to carry on her back. Someone else fastened it for her. She watched with sinking heart as the island girls began to climb the rock face. Then she saw that the cliff actually shelved into steplike ledges that rose all the way to a break in the wall of stone, an opening onto grassy tableland.

She could feel the life returning to her hands. She scrambled, glad that the basket on her back wasn't heavily laden. Once in a while someone gave her a boost from behind. They were wonderful climbers, these women. She could never have managed without them, especially here with the slime of nesting fowl and the constant splash of waves. Once she glanced down. The boats and their rowers were as small as toys. The ocean lurched and staggered like a sinking ship. Quickly she looked back. She could see clumps of pink sea thrift at the edge of the rock.

They came out on the low end of the island. From here it rose gradually toward monumental bird cliffs, the sky above them white with seafowl. The women pointed toward those heights. Lottie sidled up to Vinnie and said she thought they were supposed to play some kind of game. Then all the girls and maidens set off at a run.

Thora glanced back and shouted to her, "Skint thee!" Vinnie understood that she was to make haste, but she shook her head, and Thora ran on. Vinnie walked. She was thinking about Ma-

122

belle on that day the weather changed, how the child had taken off with the other children in the spring air, and how relieved Vinnie had felt to see her feeling well again.

Vinnie hadn't gone far when she saw the girls returning, Thora in the lead, with something aloft in her hand. All the women formed a circle around Thora. Vinnie couldn't see what they were doing, but when Thora broke free, she was crowned with a wreath of flowers. Thora whirled, one hand holding the crown to her head, the other, the First Egg.

"Queen," Lottie said. "They've made her queen of the island or of spring. I'm not sure which."

Everyone followed Thora over the dome of the island and on down toward some tumbled rock. Vinnie stood apart as they plunged on. Standing alone that way, she was probably the first of them to catch sight of the creature that bounded out of the rocks. Vinnie caught her breath. He was real, arms flailing, bearded face uplifted, and long, ungainly legs almost bare beneath a sheepskin covering.

Thora drew up so suddenly that others following close tumbled into one another. He kept on waving and running and shouting, with, of all things, a pig at his heels. A pig! The women and girls stared and drew together and stared some more.

The man's shouts were snatched by the wind and lost to the clamor of seafowl. But Vinnie didn't need to hear him. His loping gait was unmistakable. Only Mr. Powdermaker ran like that. She had never been so glad to see anyone in all her life.

twelve

"Who are these people?" he demanded.

"I don't know."

"The Stott children?"

"Fine. All well. There's a village, fourteen cottages, on a bigger island, and a church and a manse. These people have taken care of us, and others."

"Amazing! What is their language?" he asked as the women babbled and gaped at the pig.

"I don't know. There's a boy here who understands some of it. Andrew."

"Amazing!" Mr. Powdermaker exclaimed all over again. "I don't suppose you have bread?"

"The women do. Mr. Powdermaker, sir, what about Toby?"

"Toby . . . ?"

"One of Miss Covington's children who was with us."

"A lad of ten or eleven?"

"Yes, yes. You've seen him? Where is he?"

"I'm afraid . . . Of course, it might not be the same . . ."

"Brown Holland shirt, a blue waistcoat—"

"That's the lad then. I'm sorry. He washed up here on the rocks."

Vinnie kept staring at Mr. Powdermaker. Perhaps he had made a mistake and it wasn't Toby he'd seen.

"I'm sorry. I'm afraid many lives were lost."

"But he was so brave," she insisted, as if that information could force Mr. Powdermaker to change his mind.

One of the women touched Mr. Powdermaker's sheepskin and then his gaunt arm. "Shrankie," she said to Vinnie, who knew that meant thin. He needed a joop o' kelter, the woman went on. He would be given a strood. Vinnie told him they would provide him with a suit of homespun cloth.

Mr. Powdermaker bowed gravely and thanked the woman. He would welcome a suit of warm clothes.

Next the woman inquired about the pig, but Vinnie didn't know how to explain it. As far as she knew, there was no island word for *pig*.

Mr. Powdermaker remarked that she seemed to have picked up a bit of the language herself. Vinnie was shocked. Until now, she would never have thought that she could act as interpreter. She hadn't realized she had come to understand so much.

They went on to the earth house, Mr. Powdermaker's cave. A woman opened one of the baskets and pulled out a round loaf for Thora. She entered the earth house wearing the First Flowers and bearing the First Egg and the bread. When she came to a dark low entrance into a kind of tunnel, she dropped to her knees to crawl in.

"I wouldn't go there," Lottie murmured, "not for anything."

"I don't know about the tunnels," said Mr. Powdermaker, "but that cave kept me alive with shelter and food. And it gave me a number of curious objects. I should say valuable ones."

When Thora emerged again, her crown was gone. Vinnie hoped it had been left on purpose, laid carefully with the egg and the bread. She hated to think of those flowers dropped by accident and trampled in the darkness.

As soon as Thora was standing with the others, it became clear that the time had come for everyone to go to the cliffs again to collect eggs. Vinnie told Mr. Powdermaker, who said those birds had a nasty habit of squirting a vile oil at you if you weren't careful when you robbed their nests. Vinnie said she was sure the women and girls would be careful; they used and traded that oil. Mr. Powdermaker nodded thoughtfully. "So they harvest the oil," he remarked. "Tell me more about them."

First she ran after the women and pointed to Lottie and herself and Mr. Powdermaker. The women nodded. One of them drew three loaves from a basket and gave them to Vinnie.

Mr. Powdermaker devoured the first loaf in an instant and reached for another. Lottie's mouth opened wide, then shut.

"Is this your portion?" he asked.

Lottie swallowed dryly.

He turned questioningly to Vinnie.

"It's all right. We've had other food."

"But not bread," Lottie broke in. Then she flushed.

The pig came snuffling after the crumbs. It thrust its snout into Mr. Powdermaker's hand, and he fed it a tiny morsel.

Lottie gasped.

Mr. Powdermaker smiled. "This animal was my sole companion for many months. She kept me warm." He paused. "I often thought of killing her and having all that meat."

"Why didn't you?" Lottie dared to ask.

"We could both live on the birds and some fish. And she dug roots for me. She was alive, and it's a hard thing to be absolutely alone. And she likes to be sung to. Her favorite song is 'Oh, Susannah!' So I named her that."

Vinnie laughed. "Susannah! Did you really use her to stay warm?"

"Indeed I did. It's an Irish custom I've seen carried to America. I myself come from low origins, and I'm not too proud to humble myself. One must seize every opportunity to get along. So Susannah gave me her life instead of her death. And I in turn shared

126

with her whatever I gained from this godforsaken patch of land."

While he talked, Mr. Powdermaker collected his possessions to carry away.

"What's that?" Lottie asked, as he pulled an oilskin packet from the sleeve of his tattered greatcoat.

"Documents," he said. "Passports and money. I had the presence of mind to carry them with me at all times, and so had them the day we foundered. Kept treasures, you might say. And these," he added, indicating a number of stone and metal objects, "are found treasures."

Vinnie stared at the very old knife and a round stone with a hole in it, at something that looked like a metal collar, and at a bone with a design scratched into it. Treasures? Vinnie looked up in the dimness to see if he was teasing.

"Bronze," he said, fingering the collar. "This too," he said, showing her a fish hook. "I used it to advantage, and cut my catch with this ancient dagger." He was pointing with pride to the knife. "But the value of things like this is their antiquity. They will fetch a handsome price."

"You found them right here?" Vinnie asked.

"Deep inside. Most likely they're burial things."

"Oh," breathed Lottie, her eyes wide. "Dead people? I knew it must be awful in there."

"Maybe there are. Or were." Mr. Powdermaker folded the greatcoat over and over so that nothing would slip out.

Vinnie said, "But don't those things belong to these people?"

"To their ancestors, no doubt. They aren't doing anyone any good buried here." He hoisted the bundle. "Show me where the boats will come for us."

There was a sour taste in Vinnie's mouth. Was this what was called grave robbing? She swallowed. The taste remained.

As Lottie led the way back to the landing rocks, Vinnie kept glancing toward the main island. She could see the rocky peak of

Andrew's islet lost in cloud or mist. There was only the barest suggestion of a cliff beyond, but it was the closest point of land to this far island. Mr. Powdermaker couldn't have had any idea that people were so near.

"Did you fear you might never be found?" she finally asked him.

"Not at all. I never let myself despair."

She said, "Andrew has been on the island for two years."

"Two years! By Jove, that's a long time. Have there been no travelers? No ships?"

She said carefully, "He was never in the right place when they came. Landing is very hard. There's no safe harbor."

"You don't say!"

"It's what Andrew says."

"Ah," said Mr. Powdermaker, squinting seaward. "It's curious I haven't seen them fishing before."

"It's their first time out. I don't think they fish much, because all their stored food is birds. They had no mutton this year, because they had to kill too many sheep the winter Andrew came, to feed the people they saved."

"I see," said Mr. Powdermaker, as if he could see a good deal more than she had revealed. "I wonder . . ." But he kept his musings to himself.

By the time the women and girls arrived with their baskets of eggs, the boats were close to the landing rocks. The rowers scrutinized Mr. Powdermaker and the pig, which followed Mr. Powdermaker down the cliff until her short legs could no longer keep her from slipping seaward. Then she scrambled all the way up to the turf again.

Slowly he pursued her. She stood at the edge watching him with an air of perplexity, her ears flopped over her face. He coaxed and reasoned with her, and then made a lunge at her foot. Susannah lurched back. Mr. Powdermaker lost his grip on the rock, but two women kept him from falling.

At this point he decided to leave the pig on the island to fend for herself. But Vinnie and Lottie were unable to explain this to the islanders. Ropes were knotted and hurled, and Mr. Powdermaker was urged toward the pig once more. He had to climb all the way to the turf and then sit down to catch his breath. Susannah eyed him a moment. Then she walked over to him and sank down at his feet. There was a tense pause before Mr. Powdermaker hurled himself upon her. There was horrible squealing, which kept on and on while the ropes went round and the trussed pig was lowered over the water.

She only quieted when she was settled beside Mr. Powdermaker in a boat. He kept one hand on her, but his attention was riveted on the islanders and the things Vinnie told him about them. When they cleared the headland of the main island and turned into the village bay, he gasped and half rose. "By Jove!" he exclaimed. "It is!"

Vinnie waited for him to say more, but he only looked ahead and then back and ahead again.

"I never imagined we drifted so far."

"We haven't drifted," she said.

"I mean the ship, the *Roger F. Laing*. So far off course."

"You know where we are?" Vinnie was thrilled. To be somewhere known was almost like being found.

"Pretty sure. If I'm right, why, it's famous, this place."

Vinnie's heart sank. Then he must be wrong. For there would be people and ships around a famous place.

"I'll need that boy you mentioned."

Vinnie nodded. Even if Mr. Powdermaker was mistaken, it was wonderful to have a grown-up person to tell her what was needed.

He tapped the rower nearest him. "Skellay?"

The rower twisted around to face Mr. Powdermaker, gestured at the sky, and grinned.

Mr. Powdermaker sighed. "Never mind," he said. "It has to be. The funny thing is that a fellow in Glasgow tried to interest me

129

in an excursion business. He had two packets that weren't big enough for the transatlantic trade, and he wanted to use them for excursions to Skellay. I wouldn't touch the scheme. Too risky. Skellay's famous for bad weather and no harbor. And now I find I spent the winter on it."

When the boats beached, Susannah's squeals brought the islanders on the run. By the time she was untied and thrown into the shallows to make her way ashore, almost everyone had gathered on the beach.

Joel rushed into the water crying, "My pig! It's my pig!" The pig was flailing and somehow managing to gain the shore where Joel stood in the foam. "See, he remembers me."

Vinnie hustled Joel onto dry land. "See who's here!" she declared.

Joel squinted up at Mr. Powdermaker. "Is it my father?" he asked.

"Oh, Joel!" Grace buried her face in Vinnie's skirt.

"Don't laugh at him, Grace," Vinnie said softly. "He's trying to remember."

Later, when Mr. Powdermaker was taken to the manse, Vinnie and Andrew argued about how much he should be told.

"How can he take care of us," Vinnie insisted, "if he doesn't know what's been happening?"

"He might take care of you and Perry and Grace and Joel, and maybe even Lottie. But how do we know he would take care of the rest of us? No one spoke up for me from the last lot of survivors."

"But he would. He will. He's different."

The manse door opened. The pig emerged and the door slammed shut behind her.

Andrew laughed. "The islanders don't know what to make of the pig. They think Mr. Powdermaker pulled out all its hair. They do that with the first puffin they catch. The women do. All its feathers except its wings, and then they let it go."

The thought of it made Vinnie's skin crawl.

"The other puffins get curious. They all fly over the plucked one. The women just sit on the ledge taking one after another like picking berries. They take them, break their necks, and toss them in the basket."

"It's cruel. Horrible."

Andrew shrugged. "It's their way."

"Well, I hope I'm not still around to see it."

But a hideous thought struck Vinnie. What if Perry told Mr. Powdermaker about the incident with the boat hook? Maybe Mr. Powdermaker would decide to leave her behind because she had attempted to murder the young master. Isn't that what they did with criminals? Didn't they transport them to lonely islands where they could do no more harm?

When Mr. Powdermaker and Perry came out, the pig galloped over to them, followed by Kep at a watchful distance. Mr. Powdermaker, in island tweed, had trousers reaching only to his shins, and jacket sleeves above the wrists. The only garment that wasn't too small was the waistcoat, which hung on his skeletal frame. "The height of fashion," he declared with a laugh. "Perry remains the only gentleman of quality on this island."

Perry mumbled something about the fishy smell of the tweed. As usual, he shivered in the wind. Vinnie sent him an inquiring look, but he took no notice of it.

"Now," Mr. Powdermaker began expansively, "I want to eat and eat. And then, Andrew, I want you to tell me all you know about these people."

Andrew nodded. "Sir, could I ask one question first?"

"Of course, of course. Ask away."

"As you are American . . ."

"Speak out, my boy."

"I was wondering, sir, whether you have ever been to Buffalo."

"Buffalo! Upon my word, I never expected a question like that. Take me to my dinner, and we will discuss Buffalo."

131

Vinnie hung back with Perry, who hugged himself and stepped toward the doorway.

"You didn't tell him," she said. "About what happened on the pig crate."

Perry shot a glance at her and looked away. "No. It's all a jumble now. That boy . . . The boy is dead. The boy who gave me his place."

Vinnie was staggered. He meant Toby. He must have asked about him first thing, just as Vinnie had. He must have been thinking about Toby all this time, only he was too proud to let her know.

"Master Perry," she said gently, "let me bring you a suit of clothes from the village. It will keep you warm."

He looked straight at her. He didn't say no. Maybe now that Mr. Powdermaker was wearing the island homespun, Perry would see fit to dress for the weather.

She ran all the way to find Peg. By the time she managed to explain what kind of clothing she needed and brought it down to the manse, Mr. Powdermaker was holding forth in the street with the village elders.

"George," Mr. Powdermaker was saying, pointing to himself.

"George," said the five elders in unison.

"George," murmured the rest of the men and the women who formed an outer circle. The children clustered around the pig, which had dropped exhausted across Joel's grandmama's doorway.

"And you?" Mr. Powdermaker pointed to each of the elders.

"Towrie," they answered, their heads bobbing.

"All of you?" He turned to Andrew. "Ask them."

Andrew put the question, and again, as in one voice, they spoke.

"What did they say?"

"They said, 'Oh, my dear, no, we are Towrie first.' I don't know what they mean."

"Try that one." He pointed to Joel's grandpapa.

132

"That's Shewin. I know his name."

"But ask, to see how they all answer."

The elders wouldn't reply. They told Andrew the naming was out of order, and so they must remain silent.

"Ask about the next. Go ahead. Ask them."

Andrew struggled to be clear. They listened intently, and then, without hesitation, spoke all together, "Iver."

After that the naming continued, Shewin coming next, and then Rylf Dhu and Rylf Bane. Each time, all five uttered the one name together.

"Now ask them to say what land this is, what village."

Andrew did his best, but they only answered, "The village of our people." He tried again. "Oh, my dear," they responded, "it is our home."

Later on, though, when Andrew was answering Mr. Powdermaker's questions about the islanders, and they came to the infant deaths, he declared that it all fit into place. "If I'm correct about this being Skellay, and I'm sure I am, what afflicted the infants and Mabelle is lockjaw. Skellay has been ravaged by it for years, especially with newborn babies. There have been newspaper articles. A nurse was sent some years ago, but the islanders wouldn't let her attend the births. She gave an interview and said they were a godforsaken people. Newspapers pick such things up. People like to read about primitive folk cut off from the rest of the world, all the progress of modern life passing them by. Oh, I've read about them from time to time, the way they live on the bird harvest, and some special tweed. Much in demand, the Skellay cloth." He looked down at his new clothes. "I imagine all of this would fetch a pretty penny."

"They've been very good to us," Vinnie said. She glanced Andrew's way. He pressed his lips together. She dipped her head to show her disagreement.

"They must be very good, if Andrew remained with them in preference to Buffalo."

"Oh, no," blurted Andrew. "I intend to leave. I do. I want to get to Buffalo as soon as ever I can."

Mr. Powdermaker fixed his pale glance on Andrew's tense, flashing eyes. "I see," he said.

"With the next boat. I must, or they'll think me dead." He darted a look at Vinnie.

"Is there something else?" Mr. Powdermaker inquired softly. "I feel there is."

Vinnie clamped her mouth shut. It was up to Andrew.

"No," he said in a low voice. "No, nothing else." He took off down the street and disappeared around the last cottage.

There was a moment of silence. Then Mr. Powdermaker said, "He's really been here two years?"

"Longer now."

"That does seem strange," Mr. Powdermaker remarked, "considering how eager he is to reach Buffalo."

"Is there really a place called Buffalo?" Vinnie asked him.

"Why, of course. Didn't you believe him?"

"I wasn't sure. I thought it was a kind of wild cow."

"I can assure you it is a real city. Do you think Andrew is not to be believed? Not to be trusted?"

"Oh, no, I didn't mean that."

"You didn't mean that?"

If only she could run off too. Right now she would prefer to be above the village turning the rocky soil or spreading seaware. But Mr. Powdermaker had a thoughtful look. She could tell he wasn't through with her. So she tried to explain.

"After we were rescued, I was sick a long time. Then I met Andrew, and it was hard to believe what he told me. But I do. I mean, I do trust him." She was floundering, because she realized now that she must choose between Andrew and Peg, between wariness and love. And either way, she would lose someone who had become a part of her.

thirteen 🐚

Island life pressed on. For Vinnie, everything was the same, everything was different. Soon Peg would return to her cottage for lambing and milking and cheese making. Vinnie had to explain, with gestures of love and regret, that she must stay with Mr. Powdermaker and the children. Peg let Vinnie know she still had time to change her mind, for first all the woven cloth had to be finished. It had to be washed and pulled and pounded. The women joined together at this work, six or eight at a time, with a song to carry it along.

Mr. Powdermaker mourned the lack of writing materials. He wished he could record every custom, for there was money in all of this.

"Don't give anything away to the newspapers," he warned Perry and Andrew and Vinnie. "Especially you, Andrew. We must be sure to get a photograph of you before you put on civilized clothing. I'm thinking of finding someone to write a book about you."

Andrew shifted uncomfortably. "It couldn't make a book, sir. There were days and days of . . . of nothing."

"You have no idea what people want to read about and what they buy. Listen, this entire misfortune can be turned to profit."

135

Andrew cast Vinnie a look. So much for Mr. Powdermaker's caring.

The little fields and the gardens above the village were sown with last year's seed, but the pig scrambled over a wall and dug up one of the kale yards. Mr. Powdermaker tried to tether her, but she managed to slip away. This time she was caught before much damage was done, but it was clear that she was a threat to the islanders' scanty crops.

Joel and Jack were told to keep an eye on her, and for a few days they averted new disasters. Kep took up the charge too and shadowed Susannah. If the boys lost track of her, they could always call the dog and so learn of the pig's whereabouts. Other children joined in the vigil. It became a game, all of them learning to sing "Oh, Susannah!" to get her mind off kale beds and barley sprouts.

Meanwhile the tweed was finished and rolled into bolts, which the women carried to the foreshore and covered with stone slabs.

"The tacksman," Andrew said to Vinnie. "They must be expecting him. I was to go egg gathering on the far shore, but I won't risk it now. I've told them."

The islanders acted as though they couldn't understand him. This was a task for the young people, the two older boys and Thora and Andrew, a little practice on the cliff to ready them for the perilous work of the cragsmen later on.

"What?" Mr. Powdermaker declared when he understood what was to take place. "Turn them down? You can't do that. They appear to need you. It is the least you can do to repay them."

Andrew sent Vinnie an anguished glance and strode away. Later she found him in the cottage that had become his weaving home.

"Andrew?"

He didn't look up, but she could see him stiffen.

"Andrew, listen to me. Why don't we all go? At least Grace and Joel and I. Mr. Powdermaker too. That way, if anyone comes, they'll have to fetch him back. So we'll know."

Andrew thought this over. "What if he should go back without us?"

"He wouldn't if we told him. He would be on our side. You must know that."

Andrew nodded. "All right," he said. "Only listen, Vinnie, I don't want him to know about the cleit and our hidden clothes."

"Why not?"

"It's just a feeling I have. It's my secret, that's all." Then, very softly, he added, "If he stands by us, it won't matter. We won't even need those things. But if he doesn't . . ."

Kep came panting to them. After a wet greeting, he flung himself sprawling on the packed earth between them.

"Susannah must have been up to something," Andrew remarked. He stroked the dog's heaving side.

They heard shouts and cries, then a scream.

"Oh, dear," said Vinnie. "That's Joel."

The pig had managed to squeeze through the gate to the graveyard. Kep had routed her from her digging and chased her into the open, where the villagers now closed around her. By the time Andrew and Vinnie reached them, the circle of people was parting. As Susannah slipped out through a human funnel, someone gave her a whack. Joel howled.

The pig took off across the hillside, with men and women and children in pursuit. The village dogs that had been cowed into uneasy acceptance of the pig sensed that all was changed. They sprang forward.

"No!" Joel screamed. "No!"

The chasers forced the pig to turn toward the headland just beyond the bay. Why did they go on? Vinnie wondered. Didn't they realize by now that this was not the way to catch a pig?

Andrew caught up with Joel, who was furious at being held back. "They'll hurt her," he screamed. "Let me go."

Andrew said, "It won't work. They can't have a pig here."

But Joel struck out at him and broke free. It was easy to catch him again. This time Vinnie and Andrew each took a hand. They made Joel walk. They tried to talk to him, but he was sobbing too hard to hear them.

The headland burst into whiteness, seafowl hitting the green hill like a snow squall, filling the sea and the sky. Thousands of birds overhead, all shrill with alarm, blotted the sun. By the time Vinnie and Andrew and Joel reached the throng, some islanders were turning back. Others stood at the edge of the cliff. Vinnie and Andrew held on to Joel as he pushed his way through. When they looked down, they could see only the pig's hindquarters, for her head was lodged in a crevice. A little to one side sprawled one of the dogs. Its body twitched.

"Someone should finish it," Andrew said hoarsely.

Vinnie held Joel against her.

Andrew turned, stooped, and pried a large stone from the turf. He cast it down. "Ach!" he said, sounding disgusted. He pulled up another stone. "Go on," he ordered roughly. "Take Joel away from here."

Vinnie dragged Joel back. She felt someone helping. It was Joel's grandpapa who lifted Joel clear off the ground and started down with him toward the village.

As Vinnie slowly followed, Mr. Powdermaker overtook her. "A bad business," he said, shaking his head. "Stupid. And wasteful."

"She was digging at a grave."

"I know that. And they probably have some superstition about letting loose ghosts. But to drive her like that . . ."

Andrew came down to them. He didn't speak of the dog or of what he had done.

"I don't suppose they can be blamed," Mr. Powdermaker went on. "No doubt it's some kind of primitive justice." He looked at Andrew. "Any chance of getting the carcass? Lots of good meat there."

Andrew shook his head. "The sea will take it if the birds don't finish it first."

Mr. Powdermaker nodded. "Fascinating here. But I must say I won't regret leaving these people. What about you, young man?"

Andrew rubbed his hands on his trousers and stared down at his bare feet. "Their toes are different," he said. "You'll see that when we're on the cliffs. They have toes like . . . claws."

"Do they? I hadn't noticed."

"You can come with us to the other end of the island," Vinnie put in.

Andrew kept wiping his hands as if he wanted to rid them of some taint. "I don't much relish wringing the necks of those birds," he said. "I did a lot of it last year and the year before." He gazed at his open hands. "It doesn't take any kind of special fingers."

"What?" said Mr. Powdermaker in bafflement.

But Andrew didn't answer. He just shook his head.

Before they came to the village, Andrew stopped. He nodded at Vinnie. And then, while Mr. Powdermaker sank to his heels in astonished silence, they told him what Andrew had concluded after the children from the first shipwreck were left behind on the island, and after *only* children were rescued from the *Roger F. Laing*.

After a while Mr. Powdermaker asked a few questions. He made it clear that he found Andrew's claim hard to believe. "What do you think?" he finally asked Vinnie.

She pointed to Joel's grandpapa carrying Joel down to the street. She mentioned how Amy was growing into her village family, and Jamie and Gillie and Sue-Lou and Nell. They were being drawn in, taking root.

Mr. Powdermaker pursed his lips. Then suddenly he demanded, "And is that so terrible?"

Vinnie and Andrew gasped.

"If they've found homes for themselves, families?"

"But not theirs," Vinnie blurted. "Not their own."

Mr. Powdermaker's smile made Vinnie realize how ridiculous that sounded. Miss Covington's children had no homes, not anymore. Still, they were going to be placed. And the little ones were to be adopted.

"Anyway," Andrew told him, "this is no place to live. There's no future for them here."

"You're assuming there was a future where they were heading. The land of opportunity. Well, I've seen plenty of children off the ships, and I've seen them in the workhouses. And I've seen them, some of them, carried off by strangers to who knows what kind of life. And I've even seen a puny, scared thing turned back for a stronger child that could take the hardship and the punishment."

Andrew was silenced, but Vinnie spoke up again. "That's why our children have a chance. Because Mrs. Stott will regulate all of that. They'll be visited to be sure they're being treated right."

Mr. Powdermaker was nodding. "Very true. It's what Mrs. Stott intends and no doubt will carry out to the best of her ability. But Canada, all of North America, is vast. Who will travel miles and miles by train, and then across the rugged land to some frontier farm where one of these carefully selected infants has been placed?"

"You never spoke that way before."

"Yes, I have. I've not kept my doubts from Mrs. Stott. I think that's why she relied on me. I raised questions she couldn't know about. A fine lady, Mrs. Stott. But think, Vinnie. Two years in Canada watching over these children, with more to come, and then back to England. Who will visit them then?"

Vinnie couldn't say, but Andrew said, "If they grow up on this island, they can never do anything for themselves."

"And if they were old enough to have expectations like you, it would be wrong to deprive them of their new lives. Even though, as a self-made man, I can tell you the road to success is strewn with . . ."

"With what?" challenged Andrew.

Mr. Powdermaker heaved a sigh. "With questionable deeds," he said. "But it strikes me, as I look around here, that there is much virtue in these people."

Andrew leaned back. "My uncle in Buffalo is already successful. I'm sure he has never done anything questionable."

Mr. Powdermaker smiled. "Perhaps. But even Vinnie's mother knew that America had an ugly side as well as—"

Vinnie pounced on his words. "My mother? How do you know that?"

"Your aunt mentioned it."

"And you remembered . . ."

"I remembered."

It felt strange knowing that Auntie had spoken of Mama to Mr. Powdermaker. "What else did she say? About my mama."

"Oh, this and that. I was there about your cousin, making inquiries for Miss Covington. We have to be certain the relatives of the children understand the terms of assisted emigration. There have been shocking stories, children sent away and literally lost somewhere in North America or Australia. Children who had been temporarily left in workhouses or Ragged Schools because of illness in the family or a move. I've seen some of those wretched parents trying to find their lost children. They come to the shipping offices for lists of names. I've gone down the lists for some who can't read, knowing that even if I come across the name they seek, there's little hope of ever tracing the child."

Andrew and Vinnie sat lost in thought. There was nothing more to be said just then, but there was work to be done. They had to get the children ready for the trip over the island. And they must assure the families that it was only for a few days' visit.

And there was Peg to speak with. Vinnie and Andrew approached her together. They wanted to be sure she understood about the extra children and Mr. Powdermaker coming to stay for a little while. Vinnie began, gesturing and speaking in combined English and island words. Almost at once, things went awry. Peg's eyes lit up. She gave a cry, her arms flung wide.

"No, no," Andrew broke in. "No, Vinnie, she thinks you've changed your mind, that you'll go with her to be her daughter again."

Vinnie was aghast. She felt Peg, who had caught her in a hug, slowly release her, as Andrew's voice came and went around Peg's chatter. Finally they stood apart, Peg facing Vinnie, Andrew backing toward the door.

Peg still had her smile, but her eyes were wounded and full of tears. "Cuthag," she said, still smiling.

Vinnie turned to Andrew. "What . . . ?"

"Cuthag?" He thought a moment. "Cuckoo."

"Why? What does she mean?"

Andrew shrugged. "Something about the way they use other birds' nests? I don't know."

Vinnie raised her shoulder in a questioning shrug. Peg spoke in a hush, Andrew after her. "The bird that brings spring. Then it leaves. Midsummer. It flies. To the other world."

"Oh, Peg." What she had said long before rushed into Vinnie's mind, that Vinnie had come like the bird of spring and lightened Peg's heart. Vinnie reached out to her, but Peg drew herself up. She turned aside and began to pull out things to pack in her

142

basket. She told Vinnie to gather some greens. She sounded busy, a little harried, the phrases clipped and rough.

Vinnie faltered. She wanted to make things right between them.

"Come on," Andrew called from the door. "You pick the kale, and I'll talk to Joel again. Maybe I'll give him Kep to comfort him tonight."

Still Vinnie hung back. Andrew ducked his head inside again and said, "Cuckoo's greening. Maybe she meant it was a false spring."

Blinking back tears she couldn't hide from him, Vinnie grabbed a basket and thrust past him into the bright, windswept afternoon.

"Well, don't blame me," Andrew shouted at her. "I didn't call you cuthag."

"I'm not," she snapped back at him. "I'm not blaming anyone. It just doesn't make sense. Nothing makes sense here, and I'm tired of it. I'm tired of the whole island." She stalked up the hill to the kale yard, hitching up her heavy skirt so that she could vault over the wall and get away by herself for a few minutes of peace.

It was a slow trek to the far end of the island. Thora and the older boys went on ahead to find empty cleits near the coast for shelters. Joel kept calling Kep away from Andrew.

"When I tend my sheep," Andrew teased, "I'll need to borrow him back."

Joel scowled and hugged the dog to him. "He's mine for always."

"You won't be tending sheep this year," Vinnie reminded Andrew. But she could see that gloom stalked him as they drew closer to his island. Coming back like this affected Vinnie too, but in a different way. When they arrived at the hill of the cleits and saw the sheep grazing all around, a thrill of homecoming swept

143

through her. Her step quickened until, there below on the greensward, the thatch appeared. Beyond it, sedge grass like ancient hair whipped among outcroppings that seemed to Vinnie the very bones of this land.

She raced down the hill, the wind against her, holding her upright and breaking her plunge.

"Wait!" she heard. Andrew was chasing after her.

And there was a shout from Peg too. Vinnie laughed and flung herself against the wind. Tears streamed down her face; she laughed with joy.

But when she grabbed the wind wall and whirled around to the door, Peg was there ahead of her. Peg was barring the way.

Andrew said to Vinnie, "She has to do things first. For the empty house. The fire."

Grace and Joel and Mr. Powdermaker came charging down. Vinnie and Andrew grabbed the children and hushed them as Peg stepped into the darkness and stopped at the hearth. A pair of mice scuttled across the floor and dashed through the doorway, turned, and scurried back inside again.

It didn't take long for the live embers Peg had carried, wrapped in kale and wool, to start the First Fire. Soon smoke filled the cottage and began to leak through the roof hole and the doorway. Peg emerged with a bit of smoldering turf impaled on a heather root. Standing in the doorway, she waved the smokey brand. She sang a nearly tuneless lilt in a soft-rough voice.

"What's she saying?" whispered Mr. Powdermaker.

Andrew started to translate. "The house— No, the corners of the house be blessed," he said, "and over the door, and the place of fire—" Breaking off, he stood stock-still. "It's the same," he said as Peg thrust the ember first one way and then another, nearly touching the house, the wall, and lastly Mr. Powdermaker. "I know that blessing. My mother says it. In English, but exactly like that."

144

Peg moved around the low end of the cottage. A moment later she reappeared, coming from the uphill side. Down and past, she circled the house three times, while Andrew, his face flushed, recited his mother's prayer:

> God bless all corners of this house
> And be the lintel blest,
> And bless the hearth and bless the board
> And bless each place of rest.
> God bless the roof tree overhead
> And every wall of stone
> And bless the door that opens wide
> To stranger as its own.

Peg entered her cottage and deposited the ember on the hearth. Then she opened the doorway to those outside, to Vinnie and Andrew and the children, and to the stranger, Mr. Powdermaker.

"And did your mother do that circling?" Mr. Powdermaker asked Andrew.

"Of course not. That's superstition. Peg was clearing the house of things that come into it when the fire dies."

"Still, it's a striking coincidence, you knowing the island woman's saying in English." Adjusting to the darkness, Mr. Powdermaker began to look around. "A clever writer can make something of that," he said.

"I don't need a clever writer," Andrew retorted. "I need to go to America and begin my apprenticeship in Buffalo." His voice rose. "And forget this place."

"Listen, my boy, opportunities lie all about you. You must learn to recognize them, seize them. This island is a gold mine. You and I, we'll be the prospectors. We're going to dig and dig—"

"No, it's not right. It's their island. It's all they have."

"It can only help them, improve their lot. They may even get rich along with you and me. You, because you lived among them all this time; I, because I know how to turn your experience into money; and they, because people will come to see them and to buy whatever they can from them."

Andrew stood up to Mr. Powdermaker. "They know nothing of money. They would be helpless."

"Helpless? I doubt it. No, the islanders are bound to profit from the tourists. I wager I could fill a tour boat a week too, even before I sell your story."

"It's already been tried," Andrew told him. "A packet came, but the people couldn't get ashore. The weather was miserable, and so were the tourists."

"An ill-planned excursion, no doubt," Mr. Powdermaker remarked with glee. "You'll see. It can be done right, with lectures aboard and entertainment, so it won't matter if they can't land at once. And by and by they'll have your book too, to while away the time if they must wait to get ashore."

"And will there be beautiful lights?" Grace asked. "With colors in the glass?"

Mr. Powdermaker swooped her up in his arms. "Indeed there will. I give you my word."

"What's he going to do?" Joel asked.

"Send a ship here with visitors," Vinnie answered.

Joel clapped his hands. "It will be named *Argo*, won't it? And will it have music to send it along?"

"So it will," Mr. Powdermaker assured him. "A brass band. A thumping show. The island will ring with it." He set Grace down and turned to the fire. "Yes, I really think I'll do that. If the tacksman comes soon enough, it could be launched this season." Staring into the flames, he rubbed his hands. "The right vessel, advertising; say, a maiden voyage celebrating midsummer. It might do." Suddenly he turned around. "Andrew, ask the woman when the tacksman will come. She must have some idea. Andrew?"

But Andrew had left the cottage. Vinnie pictured him on the hill as she had first seen him, darting from tussock to rock like one of the surefooted sheep. And then vanishing.

As the day faded into a long, pale twilight, Vinnie found herself falling into step beside Peg. First they swept away cobwebs and dead birds. Then there were sacks to be shaken out and aired, heather to be pulled and stuffed into them, water to be fetched from the spring, and turf and dried birds from the cleits uphill. In all these tasks they had their common language, with its few words, its many looks and gestures. It felt good and right for their closeness to be restored like this.

The children raced and explored; they picked bog violets and cotton grass; they raced again until they were ready to drop. For the first time in many months, Vinnie was able to bathe them and put them to bed properly.

Mr. Powdermaker insisted that he would be fine on the floor. With Andrew. But Andrew didn't return. His absence made Vinnie uneasy, then annoyed. He seemed to go out of his way to antagonize Mr. Powdermaker. She couldn't understand opposing Mr. Powdermaker's scheme for a book about Andrew's time on the island. Wouldn't it help Andrew make up for those two lost years? Where was the harm in it?

Crawling past Peg, she snuggled against the two sleeping children. They were warm and sweet. Soon they would wear their own clothes again and have clean hair, brushed and combed; they would have bread and jam with their tea, and cake on Sundays. Did they sense this now that Mr. Powdermaker had entered their lives? They were so used to island ways it was hard to tell. Never mind, she thought, pulling them close. In a little while the island would be an adventure for them to tell. It would become a story. *Once upon a time . . .*

She was groping in a place that was dark, its breath stale and cold. She was forced to her hands and knees. She could feel the proud, delicate crown of flowers knocked askew by an overhang-

147

ing rock. Reaching up to set it straight, she grazed her knuckles on slime-covered stone. Shuddering, she pushed on toward a distant opening, a kind of graying like a promise of light.

All at once she could stand again. She had to step across bones. She didn't want to look, but she was afraid of tripping over them. Bones and a tiny egg and metal things glinting dully. And a dead pig. She was afraid, but a hand reached out to her and she landed clear, skidding on a sanded floor. Here, where it was warm and dry, the walls were wood, with small, shuttered windows. There were rafters overhead, no thatch, and from them hung sausages and bunches of dried herbs. You could smell meat over here and comfrey and tansy over there, and everywhere woodsmoke and something dark and sweet simmering in an iron pot. Exultant, safe, she ran laughing toward laughter, toward a great black hug with buttons pinching her face.

Vinnie sat up. She shivered, for here in the thin light, surrounded by stone, she could never be so warm and safe as in her dream room. Where was that magic place? She thought of pictures in storybooks, of Grace's dollhouse, of magic lantern scenes. She sank back and snuggled against the children. Maybe if she fell asleep she would find it again. Maybe she would recognize it.

148

fourteen 🦋

It was nerve-racking out where the puffins and guillemots nested. Vinnie had a horror of stepping on a puffin burrow. The fragile network of roots and wind-scoured grasses would collapse, killing birds and destroying eggs. And Joel was a constant worry. He kept trying to scramble down to the rocky ledges below. He was convinced that the pig would eventually swim around the island to find him.

Andrew, a rope around his middle, was halfway down the cliff gathering guillemot eggs. He was playing the role of islander to the hilt, living with the boys and Thora, and working the long hours of daylight.

Mr. Powdermaker chuckled. "Look at him there with the feathers in his hair. He has a knack." Andrew was bouncing off one ledge and reaching out with his bare foot for a fresh toehold. "A knack for fitting in. He'll do well in America."

Vinnie put out an arm to restrain Joel, who shrieked and tried to fling it off. "Look at the funny birds," she implored. But Joel had been seeing puffins all around him for days now. "They're tammy norries," he said.

"That's what the islanders call them. But *we* call them puffins."

"Why?"

"We just do. It's their name."

"Is tammy norrie wrong?"

Vinnie sighed with exasperation. "Just different. Like all the words they speak and we don't."

Joel said, "May I go to Peg and Grace?"

"Yes. But don't go running suddenly and scaring the sheep."

Joel called Kep and headed inland toward the vale, where Peg had already started milking ewes that had lambed early and lost their young. Each day Vinnie and the children came across more tiny corpses, little woolly rags without eyes, for the gulls and crows got at them as soon as they dropped.

With Joel off her hands, Vinnie stretched out, face down like Thora, and groped in a burrow for an egg. Turning sideways, she caught a glimpse of Mr. Powdermaker loping over the hill. He called to her.

"Quick. I saw something. On the rocks."

Vinnie scrambled to her feet and followed him. He had been walking along the edge of the cliff. And there, right there, way down on the ledge. Could she see? Vinnie peered. There was a blue-gray patch with tiers of fulmars nesting all around it. But it wasn't anything, Vinnie said. It wasn't even recognizable, just a scrap of cloth.

Yet Mr. Powdermaker couldn't seem to put it from his mind. He rubbed his face and pulled at his beard and finally plunged his hand inside his jacket and pulled out the oilskin packet. He flapped down on one knee like a scrawny seabird alighting on a rock. "I can't go on like this," he blurted. "I can't. I'm going to tell you everything. I should have before. Long since."

Mystified, Vinnie squatted down.

"Toby," he said. "I never even knew his name. He had no name, just Boy."

Vinnie nodded. Why would anyone name a dead person?

"I knew he was one of them, though. After a while, you can

tell. You recognize those faces out of the workhouses and the Ragged Schools. It doesn't matter whether they are well or dying, tough or scared—"

"He was the bravest boy I've ever known," she said.

Mr. Powdermaker made a strangled sound. Then he cleared his throat. "Thrown away," he said. "Wasted. Not you, though. You'll be all right. I'm going to see to that."

"I know I'll be all right," Vinnie answered. "It's the little ones I'm worried about."

Mr. Powdermaker waved his hand. "All of them."

"You've already done so much—"

"No!" he cut in. "I put them on the *Roger F. Laing.*"

"You couldn't know about the storm. It's not your fault."

"You should have been on a safe passenger ship. There was one bound for New York the same day."

"But we were going to Halifax. You did exactly what Mrs. Stott wanted."

Mr. Powdermaker was shaking his head. "I put you on a ship carrying railway iron, a vessel that had no business adding human cargo."

"You yourself came on it, sir. You thought it was fine."

He smiled grimly. "Yes, I had to take the chance myself. I couldn't afford to have my American connections exposed. My brother's children's home on Long Island has been profitable, even with the medical examinations. They're a sham, of course. The home is nothing but a baby farm."

"Weren't you helping Mrs. Stott reform that kind of thing?"

"Yes. While continuing it." There was an edge to his voice. "I couldn't afford to stop entirely."

Vinnie held very still. The wind off the ocean carried flecks of spindrift and feathers. "I don't know what you're saying," she told him. Her teeth began to chatter.

"You're a child. You can't know. And I don't think I myself know how much my work with Mrs. Stott was for profit and how much for conscience. But I couldn't risk her seeing me with my brother and his activities in New York. So I had to keep from her what I learned from your aunt. You see, Vinnie, you are American."

"What?" Vinnie sank back.

"A citizen of the United States. If Mrs. Stott had known, she would have insisted on trying to find your family for you."

"But my parents are dead."

"I know that. Your father was an American seaman. He brought your mother to America, and you were born in his parents' house in Brooksville, Maine."

Vinnie clutched herself. *My father was a sailor, he sailed across the sea . . .*

"Your mother hated America for what it did to her. That's what your aunt told me. Only it wasn't America, it was the governor of Massachusetts."

Vinnie shivered convulsively.

"Your father's ship was due in Boston. It was overdue. Your mother heard it was lost, with all hands. But she heard other rumors too. She went to Boston. She took you. She was expecting another child. She must have haunted the docks, poor woman. Your aunt says that she waited and hoped until her money ran out, and then she went to a shelter. It happened to be when the governor was making a sweep of the shelters, picking up people without means of support who would be a burden to the Commonwealth."

Vinnie shook her head in confusion. Commonwealth? Was a governor a kind of king? He couldn't be. There were no highnesses in America.

"Your mother and a number of other poor people who were not Americans were rushed off to England on the next available ship. You were included, of course."

"Was it a mistake?"

Mr. Powdermaker laughed. "One newspaper called it a crime.

152

You were a citizen of the country that booted you out, though you were not yet three years old."

Vinnie frowned. "My auntie told you all this?"

He nodded. "And it was confirmed. Would you like to see the proof?" He unwrapped the oilskin packet. He had to stoop over it to keep the bills and documents from flying off in the wind. When he pulled out one paper, they drew together to shield it, but even so he couldn't open it all the way. She saw at the top, "The United States of America." She saw her own name written in, a seal stamped there and last year's date and the words, Department of State.

His long finger inched spiderlike across the rattling sheet and stopped at a number. "Your own number. And this says you are to be given all lawful aid and protection." He folded the paper and slid it back inside the oilskin. "What do you think of that?"

She had no thoughts at all, not whole ones, just bits and pieces hurtling past like the spume and the feathers.

"Shall I keep it for you?" he asked.

"What?"

"Your passport."

"Yes, please." Looking down, she saw that she was kneeling on a clump of sea thrift. She moved and tried to raise the pink blossoms. "My mother had a baby," she murmured.

"It was born during the crossing. It died. Your aunt says your mother never recovered her strength after that. But I suspect she was already in poor health when she took refuge in the shelter. They were quick to expel people who were ill."

"Why didn't Auntie tell me?"

He shrugged. "Your mother didn't want you to know until you were grown. By the time I spoke with your aunt, she was so anxious about her own child, it just slipped out. It was bound to anyway, once emigration was arranged."

But it was baffling and hurtful. After all, Mr. Powdermaker was only Mrs. Stott's advisor. How could Auntie leave something so

153

important to him? And her mother dying with her secret. "Mama," Vinnie whispered, trying to imagine the misery and despair of that time at sea. Vinnie shut her eyes. She could almost picture her mama writhing on a narrow sleeping shelf, but the ship she saw was the *Roger F. Laing.* Yet a voice came to her, not Mama's, but the voice of a kind stranger: "Poor little thing . . ." There was a soft, warm muff. It was real, that muff, more real to her through all those years than her ailing mother and the baby. "Poor, poor Mama," Vinnie said.

"Yes. She must have been a bitter woman."

Vinnie said almost angrily, "If only I'd known."

"Well, at least you do now. Maybe you'll find your grandparents."

Vinnie's scrambled thoughts hadn't taken her that far. "Is it possible?"

"Certainly possible."

"Oh, thank you," she cried. "Thank you, thank you."

"Hold on. I don't even know if they're alive or still there. I gather your mother or someone in Boston sent word to them, for help. Your aunt wasn't sure who tried to reach them. All she knew was that they weren't heard from in time."

"Where is it?" Vinnie asked. "I've forgotten. Oh, what if I forget again?"

"Brooksville, in Maine. I believe it's a village somewhere near Searsport. Fishing and farming, I should guess, and timbering."

"Oh." She didn't know what that meant—*timbering*—but it sounded grand.

As they started back toward the egg gatherers, Mr. Powdermaker talked about Toby. He had found the boy still alive, but couldn't get him up onto dry land. He had watched him die.

They could hear the thin wail of a lamb, insistent, high. A sheep circled nervously by a clump of heather.

"Couldn't get him to land, then afterward I couldn't get him

154

into the sea either. I'd find him in rock pools. Day after day. Or caught in seaweed on the tide." Mr. Powdermaker scanned the horizon. He wouldn't look at Vinnie. "I prayed for forgiveness from him, from every child I ever brought away. I had to stone the pig to keep her off. I swore that if I lived . . . By Jove! What's that?"

Following his gaze, Vinnie caught sight of a cloud of gulls. Then she saw the boat beneath them. "The tacksman!" she cried.

"Maybe," he said. "No, I don't think so. Looks like a fishing smack. Riding low in the water. It must have a full load."

"Can we signal it?"

"They won't notice, not at that distance. And they're heading wrong, unless they mean to go around the long way to the village."

"That's right!" Vinnie exclaimed. "That would avoid all the stacks and skerries. They must be coming in. We have to get Andrew. And Grace and Joel."

Vinnie was ready to fly, but Mr. Powdermaker drew her up. They weren't sure the boat was heading in, or how long it would stay if it did, or how much room it might have for unexpected passengers. If he set off for the village at once, he had the best chance of meeting the fishermen, even if only to send word for help. The important thing was not to miss the boat.

That made sense. Vinnie pointed the way. "Go along till you see the little huts, then turn your back to them. You'll see the path."

He nodded. "If we can get away on this boat, I'll send word. Be ready. Alert Andrew. Have the children with you."

"Yes, we'll come right along."

"No need to raise false hopes, though. If they can take us, you'll be sent for. Otherwise, there's no hurry."

She watched him take off, his thin legs protruding from the flapping homespun, his arms flapping too. He looked like a gawky fledgling trying to take wing. Vinnie couldn't help laughing at the sight of him.

She turned and started down the vale. *My father was a sailor,* she chanted inside her head. All this long time there had been a place she belonged to, a family. "America?" She spoke softly, almost with embarrassment, like someone trying out a forbidden word for the first time. "America," she said again, still shakily, but daringly too.

Joel sprang up to meet her. Peg's limbs creaked as she slowly straightened. She made the hushing gesture lest Vinnie startle the sheep. Breathless with joy, Vinnie spun Joel around with her, and caught up Grace as well. Peg frowned, but Vinnie grabbed her too. Joel and Grace thought they were playing Ring Around the Rosie, but Peg didn't know that game and had sheep to tend.

So they danced around her instead, turning the game into London Bridge. Only Peg refused to be caught and stepped right through their locked arms. She clucked and shook her head, but her eyes were shining and chased the frown away. "What's wrong with you?" she asked in her language.

"Everything," Vinnie answered. "Nothing."

"What?" asked Peg, her face screwed up in bewilderment.

"I love you!" Vinnie exclaimed. "Oh, Peg, I love you so!"

Two days passed without word from Mr. Powdermaker. Vinnie couldn't bear not knowing about the boat; she wanted to go to the village.

But Andrew was cautious. He didn't want the islanders to think he was anxious. "If it makes you feel better, you go on ahead. They'll want you to carry eggs anyhow. We'll all be coming soon." Then he said, "Being here isn't what worries me. It's what happens next when they expect me to go to the island."

"If it comes to that, you'll just have to give up seeming ordinary. Mr. Powdermaker will stand by you."

Andrew gave a short laugh. "Yes, and that ledger in his head will be jotting down just what I owe him for it, you can be sure."

"He's not like that, Andrew. I mean, well, part of him is. But the part that grieved over Toby, that part is different."

"Which part of him," Andrew asked her, "kept your being American from you?"

Vinnie gave up. Whenever she listened to Andrew, she found herself troubled by uneasy recollections, like Mr. Powdermaker wrapping up those earth-house things that would fetch a handsome price. Still, he had convinced her of his remorse; she could practically imagine him turning his island profit to the aid of the shipwrecked children. It was so very complicated. What it came down to was that they were depending on him. They had to believe in him. She said, "I'll go back. I shouldn't stay away from the other children too long."

Andrew helped Peg adjust the basket of eggs. They placed wads of wool on Vinnie's shoulders to keep the ropes from cutting her. She wondered aloud whether this was the last time she would see Peg. This brought a sharp warning from Andrew. Vinnie must be careful, casual. Understanding the need, she was grateful for the busyness of the egg basket and the children about her. Yet at the end, Vinnie couldn't help feeling that Peg guessed something. She kept fussing with the children and putting off the hug that Vinnie, clumsy with the basket on her back, attempted. Peg turned away first; it was she who left Vinnie, as if she too were heeding Andrew's instructions to be careful and casual.

Joel tried dragging Kep by the scruff of his neck. Kep dropped to his belly. Gently, his mouth closed on Joel's wrist. Joel swung at Kep.

"None of that," snapped Vinnie. "Don't force him. Give him time to get used to you."

"How long will it take for him to like me?"

"That depends on how you treat him, doesn't it?"

Joel twirled the black-and-white ruff in his fingers. Then he got up and bounded after Grace, who was already far ahead on the track, eager to see her village friends again.

The bay was empty. Vinnie wasn't surprised. She didn't really think a fishing boat would stay long. Still, it was a letdown. She was bound to feel better as soon as Mr. Powdermaker told her that by now or by tomorrow, the outside world would have news of them.

Grace and Joel went right off in search of the other children. Amy, the first to appear on the street, stopped when she saw Vinnie. Vinnie waved. Amy lifted a hand. Gladness surged in Vinnie. Amy had missed her. That was good.

She didn't feel anything at all coming down into the village. There was none of that sense of homecoming she'd had going to Peg's. Her mind was on the fishing boat, the tacksman, on Mr. Powdermaker's news. With great care she lowered the basket of eggs to the street. Joel's grandmama helped her. Nell and Sue-Lou came along, and Vinnie, still kneeling, held her arms out to them. They came, hand in hand, to stand within the circle of her arms, but their faces told her nothing. Gillie and Jamie were with the village children, with Grace and Joel in their midst.

"Where is Mr. Powdermaker?" she asked.

They didn't know. Jack appeared lugging a fresh wooden box, a gift from the fisherman or the sea.

"Where's Mr. Powdermaker?" she asked again.

Jack glanced at the others, then looked at her. "Gone."

Vinnie told herself, *Casual, careful.* "Up the hill? With the men? Where?"

Jack trudged on, depositing the box in front of a cottage and then straightening. "With the man in the boat."

Vinnie held very still. She could hear the surf pounding in her ears, pounding and pounding, though way below them the village bay stretched to the horizon, creased but flat. "Are you sure?" The words were choked, compressed.

158

Jack cocked his head. He didn't understand her question. Perhaps he hadn't heard it.

"Are you certain?" she roared, and all the children drew together the way they had that day when she lost her temper over the hymn.

"Yes," Jack finally answered in a small voice. "I seen him. Him and Master Perry."

"Perry too!" Stricken, her hands fell to her sides. "Where? Did you see which direction?"

She saw in his bafflement the senselessness of her question. He turned seaward and pointed. She followed with her eyes. The sea was a soiled bedsheet, wrinkled, gray.

Vinnie walked over to Jack, took him by the shoulder, and turned him back to face her. "You let them? You didn't try to stop them? Do you want to stay here for the rest of your life?"

Jack shook his head.

Suddenly she pulled him to her, hugged his head against her. After a little while she released him. "Mr. Powdermaker— Did he say anything? A message?"

Eyeing her warily, Jack nodded.

"For me? Jack, tell me."

Still keeping his eye on her, Jack told her that Mr. Powdermaker had written something on the tobacco wrapper. Lottie had it. Jack told Vinnie how the boat had come and turned as if to go out to sea again, and then had dropped anchor. Mr. Powdermaker was waiting on the beach. He practically pushed the men into one of the rowing boats to fetch the fisherman ashore.

The fisherman brought tobacco for the islanders and biscuits for the children. The biscuits were all bits and pieces, but they tasted grand. Mr. Powdermaker tore the wrapping from the tobacco. The fisherman gave him something to write with. Mr. Powdermaker made Lottie wait for the wrapping, and then he and Perry got in the rowing boat with the fisherman and went out to the boat. Lottie was cross because she didn't get any biscuits.

She would probably tell miss that they didn't save any, even though Jack had tried. He had tried awful hard, but by the time Lottie caught up, all he could do was give her his hand to lick.

Vinnie just stood there.

"Honest," Jack said. "It wasn't my fault."

"I know." She had to clear her throat. "I know it wasn't." She felt as though she could go on standing there all day. What did anything matter? There was nothing she could do, no one to turn to.

Suddenly she was aware of faces in doorways, men and women watching her. Now Grace ran to one of the women and was taken into welcoming arms. *And bless the door that opens wide to stranger as its own.* It was all so natural, Grace running, the arms extended, the clasping. It struck Vinnie all over again how hard it was to tell. Was she a prisoner? Was Grace? Were Joel and Jack and Amy and Nell and the other little ones? She thought of all the stories of dungeons, of cold, dark cells with rats. Her eyes traveled from doorway to doorway, from face to face. They were deeply interested in her, but whether from craftiness or concern, she had no idea.

She knew she had to control her anger. She would turn the children from her, into the arms that opened wide to strangers as their own. It wasn't over yet, for the bolts of tweed still lay heaped on the foreshore awaiting the tacksman.

Lottie appeared in the late afternoon. She came straight to Vinnie and led her into the cottage where, in a chink in the stone wall, she had tucked away Mr. Powdermaker's oilskin packet. Inside it Vinnie found her passport as well as Joel's and Grace's, three pound notes, and a message scribbled on brown wrapping paper: *No room for more than one or two. Perry and I going. Will get word at once to Stotts, etc., to speed rescue. Tell Andrew to prepare islanders for tour boat. Have them ready souvenirs to sell to tourists. G. P.*

160

Vinnie read it in the dimness of the cottage and then took it outside to read again.

Lottie, at her elbow, said, "Did you ever see so much money?"

Absently Vinnie shook her head. She was trying to decide how to have the children ready for the tacksman. There was the cleit with clothes the children might need, especially the little ones. And Andrew. Especially Andrew, now that Mr. Powdermaker was gone. Only Andrew didn't want her to let anyone know about that clothing, not yet. But what if the tacksman came before Andrew returned? Would it be too late then to dress up the little ones and get them onto the tacksman's boat? After all, once he was here, Andrew could speak for himself. It wouldn't matter what he was wearing as long as he was able to identify himself, as long as he could talk to the tacksman.

Vinnie decided to wait. She had promised Andrew to keep his secret. But she would explain to Jack and Lottie how important it was to keep track of every child, to be ready to leave.

"Find Jack," she told Lottie. "You two meet me in the school-room."

"When?"

Vinnie looked down to the bay. There was a yellowish haze at its rim. The day was old. Soon it would sink beyond the horizon, and night would barely spread its gray wings before the next day came thrusting and clamorous with waking seafowl. "Now," she said. "Right now."

She went on ahead to give herself a chance to sort out what she would say to them. But inside the manse she stood at a loss. If she alarmed Lottie and Jack, the islanders would soon find out. She would have to be careful, casual.

Something like a step sounded in the other room. Something dropped on the floor in there. Footsteps padded.

"Jack?" she called. "Is that you?"

The door opened. It was Perry, shoes in hand.

"But you went!" she cried. "Jack said so."

"And came back," Perry said. "I got all the way out to the boat. I thought about leaving Grace and Joel. I couldn't."

"Oh, Master Perry, I'm so glad." She beamed at him.

He had the beginning of a smile as he added, "Besides, it was all fish. Fish on the decks, fish in the hold. Fish."

"But I'm so glad," she said again. And then everything came tumbling out of her about the children and Andrew and the cleit, and how they must have the necessary things at hand, but not a moment too soon lest they alert the islanders and lose some of the little children.

Lottie and Jack ran in together, eager for an adventure. They knew Vinnie was planning something for them to do. But Perry took command. "You know the tacksman is coming any day now."

They nodded.

"You know that he may not be able to stay very long because the harbor is unsafe, so it's important that you be ready to leave." He spoke sternly and slowly. "It's especially important that we have all the little ones ready as well."

They looked at him in silence. They could sense that there was more to what he was saying. They waited.

Perry shrugged at Vinnie. "What else?" he seemed to be asking.

"Maybe," Vinnie suggested, "each of us should be responsible for certain little ones."

Perry said, "I don't know which is which."

"Me and Lottie, we'll divide 'em up," Jack offered.

Vinnie took on the two Stott children and Nell and Sue-Lou, Jack took Gillie and Jamie, and Lottie took Amy. They decided on a secret meeting place—the graveyard. They promised one another not to discuss any of this in front of the islanders, for, as Vinnie pointed out, they could often be understood, even when the language they spoke was not. Perry didn't think the islanders were bright enough to pick up things like that, but if it made Vinnie happy to turn this into a conspiracy, he wouldn't interfere.

It was done then. They had their plan. When Andrew came back, he would decide how and when to move the clothing nearer to the village. All they had to do now was wait and watch, to keep on with their tasks and games and meals as though nothing out of the ordinary was about to happen.

fifteen 🦋

But the waiting was hard. It was hard not to stare out to sea, hard not to glance up the track to see if Andrew was coming. At first she tried to stay away from Perry so as not to arouse suspicion. It didn't occur to her that a resumption of lessons would have been normal. She just decided finally that she had to do something, and sent the children down to the manse for a singing lesson.

They began with a hymn they all knew, "Awake, My Soul." The inside door opened and Perry came through into the schoolroom. She cast a smile in his direction, singing "A heavenly grace demands thy zeal, and an immortal crown, and an immortal crown." Her head swiveled around for another look at him. He was wearing a proper suit of clothes. Even with his shaggy head of hair, he looked like a young traveler.

Aghast, she told the children they had sung beautifully and could now go. They didn't want to. They had just begun. They wanted to sing some more.

"Tomorrow," she promised. "We'll have a long lesson tomorrow." She waited until they had all left, and then faced Perry. "You went to the cleit. You had no right."

164

"No right?" He yanked each short sleeve down. "Whose decree, Miss Highness?"

"Andrew's counting on that suit."

"He'll be fine. He's used to dressing like a herdie boy."

"You don't understand."

"I understand that if I'm to command attention and respect with the tacksman, if I'm to act in authority on your behalf, on everyone's, I'd better present the right appearance."

"Perry," she said, deliberately dropping the *Master*, "the cleit was a secret. Andrew's secret. I promised—"

"If you broke your promise, you must work that out with Andrew. But don't be so childish over what needed to be done if I'm to be treated according to my station."

Vinnie's throat ached. "If the islanders see you like that, they'll know we've found the hidden clothes."

Perry shrugged. "What can they do about it?"

"Move them. Hide them."

"They're much too busy to worry about a little clothing. Anyway, no one sees me except the old man who brings food, and he's mostly out of his head. You're making a fuss over nothing."

Vinnie wanted to believe him, but as soon as she walked away from the manse she could hear Andrew saying that Perry always had to be better than everyone else. And so he was now. But at what cost?

That night when Peg's parents-in-law were snoring comfortably in their bed cupboard, Vinnie crept out of the cottage. She had to hurry, because no one slept very much when the nights were so short.

She heard something moving behind her. She knew from adventure stories that you were supposed to lead your pursuer astray and cover your tracks. There wasn't time for that sort of thing. She needed every minute of darkness she could get.

Before she crested the first rise, her pursuer came abreast of her. It was Kep, his eyes gleaming, his tail brushing against her skirt. She was so relieved she gave herself a moment to catch her breath. Then they were off, side by side this time. It was a good feeling. The run across this narrow end of the island could seem interminable when every dip and every rounded hillock looked the same.

The cleits looked the same too. She came to them quite suddenly, for the dim night distorted shapes and space, and from a distance they had the look of boulders that had pushed their way out of the earth and were still capped with the turf that had once buried them.

She knew better than to bother checking the first cleits. But as she passed one and then another, she grew unsure. She tried to count without starting over. Never mind counting, she decided, when that didn't work. She would just glance inside each one.

She started with a cleit that contained a few dried seabirds, another with ropes and sacks. The next one, she thought. But it was empty. And the one after it was empty as well.

She made herself slow down. No need for panic. She would just have to be methodical. This one, for instance. But it was empty too. Or was it the one she had already looked in? Maybe Kep would remember that bitter day with Andrew and lead her to it. She turned and turned. The sky over the sea was growing light. She was thankful for the darkness on the land.

She stayed as long as she dared, going from one cleit to another. Again she found baskets and ropes and sacks. In an otherwise empty cleit, she came across a dead lamb still wrapped in its birth membrane. At last she gave up and started back to the village. She knew there was no chance of having missed that cleit among the others in the cluster.

By the time she got back, a light rain was falling, the gray horizon shutting in the island. She wasn't noticed. But then it no longer mattered. The islanders had seen Perry, and they had moved the clothes and the chest and all its wonderful contents.

By midmorning she couldn't keep her eyes open. The men's pipe smoke was sweet and thick in the soggy air. She crawled into the empty bed cupboard, drawing her cold feet under her skirt. But she felt clammy and weighted with filth. She had planned to bathe the little ones in the ebb shallows before dressing them for their journey. Maybe she should tell Lottie and Jack where she was. What if they suddenly needed her? But she couldn't stir.

When she woke, she thought she was at Peg's. The silence was intense. She swung her feet to the floor, then quickly drew them back. She saw now that she was in the village. But where was everybody?

Out in the street, she looked up the path first, then downhill. There they were, outside the manse. Her first thought was that they were going to the church. Then her gaze swept on down to the bay. There was a boat. She knew it must be anchored, but the gray of sea and sky pressed in on it. Never had anything seemed so unconnected, so adrift.

At the manse she couldn't get through the crowd to the tacksman, but she heard Perry speaking over the uproar. "All of us," he was saying, and he sounded convincing, commanding, "every single child." She drew a deep breath. It was all right. Perry was handling the situation just as he had planned.

She was put to work with the women and girls carrying supplies from the beach to the village. Oarsmen rowed back and forth to the anchored boat. Other men directed the temporary storage of crates and barrels and full sacks. The elders surrounded the tacksman; they argued, demanded, wheedled. The tacksman held up four fingers to the elders and pounded four times on the wall. Vinnie was kept too busy to see how the bargaining came out. Anyway, now that Perry had taken charge, all she needed to know was when the tacksman planned to leave.

She drew Jack aside and asked him what he had heard. He was sucking a sweet. He was absolutely happy. She stopped Lottie on

167

her way back to the shore. "Someone has to get Andrew," Vinnie said to her. But Lottie was quite sure Andrew and the others had already been sent for. They were needed for the tacksman.

That evening there was a feast, with meat and tinned fruit, spirits for the grown-ups and sweets for the children, and tea, wonderful tea. Vinnie thought of Peg alone at the other end of the island. At least the boys and Thora would be home before the tacksman left. Peg wouldn't get to taste any of these treats.

Thora and the boys arrived with eggs for the tacksman's boat. The next lot would be carried to the village cleits. But before that, first thing tomorrow morning, the young people must fetch the feathers baled and stored on the near island.

As soon as Vinnie understood this, she made her way to Andrew, who was gobbling meat and bread. "Don't go," she whispered urgently.

Even with his mouth full his voice was easy. "They notice when you whisper. Careful and casual, remember?"

"Mr. Powdermaker went with the fisherman."

The bread stopped midway to his mouth. Then he said evenly, "I'm not surprised."

"There wasn't room on the boat. He left a note. Anyway, Perry has spoken with the tacksman. He's arranged for us all to be taken."

"Go on. That's not all."

"No." And then she told Andrew about the clothes. She told him everything.

He grew quiet. Then he told her where to find her skirt and cloak.

She said, "But we won't need them now. I've just told you. Perry has spoken for us."

"Just in case," he said, "get them. Promise."

"All right." She would do anything to make up for giving away his secret. She told him about their meeting place, and said she

168

would bring the skirt and cloak there. Or to him. Whatever he wanted.

"I won't be here," he said. "I'll be fetching the feathers."

"No, Andrew. You've just come back. Why should you go again?"

He leaned over to wipe his fingers on a clump of grass. "For one thing, I was there the whole time last year. And after. I know where every bale is. For another, I'll end up unloading them on the tacksman's boat, as we'll bring them straight there. They say there's fog coming. The tacksman wants to be on his way while he can still see."

"Oh," said Vinnie with relief, "that's a perfect plan."

Andrew scowled. "I know. Too perfect. After all those other times . . ."

"There's more of us looking out for each other this time."

Andrew nodded, his glance shifting from her to the faces nearby. "They're watching us, though. I can tell."

"They know you're leaving. They'll miss you."

Andrew sighed. "If that's all it is . . ." His words trailed off. "All the same," he finished, "I wish I had the jacket and trousers."

"I could speak to Perry again."

"Don't waste your breath. Only if something happens . . . if I'm delayed, you'll have to speak for me."

"Of course I will. But you won't be. You'll be delivering the feathers. You'll be staying right there on the tacksman's boat."

"Yes. I don't know. It just seems too smooth." He looked around again. "We should separate now."

She nodded, then suddenly shivered. She felt his uneasiness. She wished she could have Grace and Joel to sleep with her that night. But she had to give up the idea, for later on she would have to go and fetch the skirt and cloak that Andrew had buried a second time. Yes, and hide them inside the graveyard wall, the place of last resort.

When Vinnie got up the next morning and saw the thickening fog, she knew at once she had to talk Andrew into staying. But she was too late. Andrew and the others had left before dawn. There was only the one remaining rowing boat to carry the oil and tweed to the tacksman's boat.

The day dragged. The villagers bent to the carrying and hauling with uncanny silence. Vinnie had the children play The Sea Is Rough, until Amy suddenly asked if they were about to be tipped over into the sea again. They sang "Oh, Susannah!" They sang hymns and carols until they were hoarse. And the silence in the village only deepened. Once or twice a mama or grandpapa paused just long enough to touch one of the children. Vinnie kept telling them they could say their good-byes on the beach, where eventually all of the village gathered. The children didn't seem to understand. They looked up into faces rigid with grief and streaked with tears. Vinnie thought of Peg and turned away.

When Perry came striding down to the rowing boat, Vinnie pushed forward to stop him. It was too soon, she said. Andrew wasn't back yet. The feathers hadn't been loaded.

But just then the rowing boat appeared from around the headland. It was stacked with bales. It headed straight for the anchored boat. Vinnie craned for a glimpse of Andrew. She saw two oarsmen—two oarsmen and no one else.

"Vinnie." Joel tugged at her.

"Just a minute."

"Vinnie!"

"Oh, what is it?"

"Where is Kep? Isn't he coming with us?"

"Kep? No. No, Joel, he has to stay here."

"But he's mine."

"Oh, Joel, for goodness sake, I can't think about that now. I'm worried about Andrew coming."

"Will Andrew bring him then?"

"Joel, please! It's hard enough without a dog too." She glanced

170

down at Joel's troubled face. "Please, dear Joel, hush for now. And stay right with Grace."

She dashed from one person to another. She spoke Andrew's name, asking. Each gave her a tearful nod or a loving smile. They pointed with sweeping gestures toward the island. Then she ran to Perry to tell him the tacksman must wait for Andrew.

Perry shook his head. "He's already said he's not pleased at the prospect of so many unexpected passengers. Earlier he was talking about other boats having to come. I'm not sure. I thought I had made it clear to him, that he'd agreed. But he has such a queer way of speaking. He's more like the islanders than us."

"Then I'll speak to him myself. One of us has to."

"I should. I will. How I wish I'd never gone to that hut. I thought I was doing the right thing."

"If you can just delay him . . ."

"Yes. I'll try." He climbed into the rowing boat.

The oarsman waited for more passengers, so Vinnie gestured at Lottie. She and Amy could go out to the boat now too.

"What about me?" said Jack.

"Yes, all right, you and the little boys."

"I'll just get them," he said, but as he turned away, the oarsman pushed off.

The bales of feathers were still being stowed when Perry climbed aboard. She saw him approach the tacksman. Perry was pointing. It looked to Vinnie as though the tacksman was shaking his head. Then Perry climbed onto the foredeck. Cupping his hands to his mouth, he shouted across the water.

"Can you hear me?"

"Yes."

"He doesn't believe me about Andrew." Perry's voice broke. "I mean it, Vinnie. He really doesn't, and I can't delay him. He says he must be away from here because of the fog."

"Tell him I want to speak to him."

Perry called the tacksman to the foredeck.

"There's another boy," Vinnie yelled at the top of her lungs. "On the island."

The tacksman spoke, but his accent and the noise all around prevented her hearing him.

"Did you hear that?" Perry called.

"No."

"He says he's already overloaded. He can't take all the children this trip anyhow. He says he'll send another boat. He says he'd make trouble with the islanders if he took off one of their lads."

"Explain!" she screamed at Perry.

"I did. He thinks Andrew just wants to get away. He saw the boys leave this morning. He's sure Andrew's one of them."

The tacksman shouted something else.

"What?"

"He says twenty or so went away to Australia a few years back. If more leave, the islanders will be ruined."

"Aye," the tacksman shouted, "they need the young lads for cragsmen, for their living."

Vinnie was at a loss. She realized now that any lad who had gone to show the others where the feathers were must seem an islander. Maybe the tacksman would listen to her argument if they weren't shouting across the water. Maybe, if they spoke face to face, he would believe her. Only if she went out there, mightn't he just take off?

She glanced back to locate the children. There were Nell and Sue-Lou and Gillie and Jamie. There was Grace and—

"Grace!" Vinnie shrieked. "Where's Joel?"

"He went for Kep."

"No!"

"Please, miss," said Jack. "I saw him when I was after Jamie. He says he won't go without the dog."

"Whyever didn't you stop him?"

"You told me to fetch the little boys."

172

She had to find Joel. At least Jack was still here to keep the rest of the little ones together. But she would have to bring Grace along with her to be sure the boat stayed. Perry would never let the tacksman start without her.

"Watch the little ones," Vinnie told Jack. "If there's any change, anything at all, you come for me."

"Where, miss?"

"You know."

"Oh, that place. And will you be there too?"

"I don't know where I'll be," she cried. "I'll be looking for Joel."

"You'll not find him. He's ever so good at hiding."

Yanking Grace after her, she tore up the path. Grace began to cry. Vinnie had to drag her all the way around the manse to avoid being seen boosting her over the graveyard wall.

"What are we doing here?" sobbed Grace. "I don't want to be here."

"Hush. Darling Grace, do be good. Please."

"Aren't we going with Perry and Lottie?"

"I have to find Joel first."

"Joel's not coming. He told me. He's gone far away."

Vinnie made Grace promise to sit against the wall without uttering a single word. Then she clambered back on the uphill side and ran to the village. She called Joel and she called Kep. She heard the tacksman's boat horn, three sharp blasts. She knew they were to summon her. She ducked into one cottage after another, calling, calling. She stumbled uphill, shouting across the kale plots and into the fields. Then she pelted down the hill again to the graveyard.

Andrew was there with Grace. He had crossed the channel as soon as he could, as soon as he realized from the way they loaded the rowing boat that the oarsmen never intended to bring anyone with the feathers. While the other boys had begun to set their ropes on the crags to begin the fowling, Andrew had slipped away. The tide was wrong. It was rising. So he had to plunge in, to swim for his life, and then run for it. All this way.

He was still soaked. He lay panting and spent, while Vinnie told him where everyone was, and was not. He stretched out in the rough grass. "Then I have to stay after all. For Joel." He drew himself up. "At least they'll send for him."

Vinnie's thoughts were spinning a thread of an idea. She grabbed the skirt and cloak and dropped them in front of Andrew. "Put these on," she said.

"What, these? No, Vinnie, I can't."

"You've worn women's things before. Remember?"

There were three blasts on the horn again, longer and louder.

"That was different. I had no choice."

"Nor do you now. You know I can't leave Joel. You be me. Take Grace. The tacksman's so anxious to go, he won't notice."

But Andrew just sat there.

"Hurry, Andrew. You must get away while you can."

"And if you should need the cloak after I'm gone?"

She thrust it at him. "I'll be fine. I have my passport. And Grace, you must talk to Perry as soon as the rowing boat gets near."

"What should I say?"

"Just talk. Very fast, until Andrew is on board and you are all under way."

Andrew shook his head. "Perry will see. He'll give me away."

"Perry will see, and he won't give you away. The talk is to distract the tacksman."

Andrew shook his head. "I don't like it. I don't like him."

"You don't have to like him. Or," she added, her eyes flashing, "be like him."

"What?"

"So sure of your own opinion you can't hear any other. Perry knows he did wrong. He won't give you away."

174

Andrew reached for the cloak, then stopped, his hand suspended, making a fist. She touched the hand, feeling how hard it was, how cold. His fingers opened and for an instant gripped hers. She said, with a smile coming into her voice, "Think what a surprise it will be for Perry."

"What surprise?" Grace wanted to know. Andrew shook out the skirt and climbed into it.

"It's like a play," Vinnie told her. "Remember when your cousins came, and we all acted a play and had an announcer and theater curtains?"

"They weren't real curtains; they were my coverlet. And Daisy wore mother's dressing gown."

"That's right. Daisy was the queen. Now," Vinnie declared with a laugh, as Andrew stood in the falling mist with the cloak draped about him, "Andrew is playing a part too, and you mustn't give him away. You must call him Vinnie."

"Vinnie!" Grace repeated. She laughed. "That will fool everyone."

Jack came slamming through the gate, breathless, and when he caught sight of Andrew, wide-eyed.

Vinnie cried, "Joel's back? He's come back?"

Jack, open-mouthed, shook his head.

"Then what are you doing here? You're supposed to stay with the little ones."

"That's just it," he answered, his eyes riveted on Andrew in the skirt and cloak. "They took 'em back. First they were just standing there and crying. Then the man on the boat said something, and then they did, they took 'em back."

Vinnie shot a glance at Andrew. She knew he was thinking what she was. If they tried to collect the little ones now, the tacksman would refuse them anyway, and Andrew was sure to be discovered.

Jack said, "Master Perry says, as there's no room, I'm to stay. Must I stay, miss?"

175

Vinnie's lips formed: Joel!

Andrew said, "Jack's far too big to pass for him."

The fog was turning to rain. Jack wiped his dripping hair from his eyes. "Please, must I?"

The horn blew again.

"Under the cloak," Vinnie said, already untying her shawl and unfolding it to the oilskin packet. She pulled out Grace's passport and two pound notes. These she handed to Andrew.

He stooped to roll them up inside his wet trouser legs. While his head was lowered, Vinnie spread the shawl over it and tied it in front. She pulled it way over his forehead, until his face was all but hidden. Then she placed Grace's hand in Andrew's.

"Jack, underneath here," Andrew told him. "Quick. I'll put my arm around you. How's that?"

Even through the fog and rain, it didn't fool Vinnie, but it was now or never. The horn was blasting away. Perry was shouting from the anchored boat. "Run," she instructed. "Stick close together. Don't stop for anything."

But once they were out on the path, Grace twisted around. "Don't look back," Vinnie called to her. Then she shrank against the wall, willing herself to blend with the gray homespun and the gray stone and the gray land in the clutches of sea and sky drained of color—all gray.

sixteen ❧

At first everything Vinnie did was charged with energy and purpose. She moved the children into Perry's room. Little Jamie was so miserable, though, that she gave in, gave him up. Sue-Lou and Nell kept leaking away to the village whenever they could, but she brought them back, day after day, night after night. It was a struggle in which the islanders took no active part, or so it seemed. They neither protested when the children were moved, nor refused them when of their own accord they returned to the cottages.

But as the days stretched into weeks, the constant pressure wore Vinnie down. While the islanders went about their work, Vinnie was left in a world bounded by views of the bay and nearly continuous hours of daylight. She found herself thinking over Mr. Powdermaker's question: Was it wrong to uproot these children again when they seemed to be thriving in families that had opened wide their doors to them? Maybe the children would tell her, in some fashion all their own, whether they should remain or leave. Yet how could they? There were no clues here, no reminders of another life.

At least not for them. But Vinnie came across the remnants of a kitchen garden behind the manse. Someone had planted herbs there where they would be out of the wind and had walled them with beach stones. The children saw no difference between these plants and all the others growing everywhere around them. Vinnie could not give up. She rubbed thyme between her fingers; the children breathed in the lemony scent without a spark of recognition.

She wondered about the salvaged things from the shipwrecks. If she dared lose sight of the bay, she would look for them in cleits on other parts of the island. She imagined having the magazine page, the ledger. Every word and number would be as enthralling as a tale from *The Heroes*.

She read the Bible to the children, but only Joel was able to memorize passages with her. He kept asking when they would see Grace. She had to warn him about running off again. If he wanted to see Grace soon, he must always be within call.

The wind was wild the day a boat finally did appear. Vinnie gathered all of the children. They had practiced holding hands and setting forth at her command. She brought them all the way down to the beach, a few of the village children in tow. The boat tacked toward the bay, but couldn't beat in against the wind. It heeled and wallowed and was swept dangerously close to the rocks at either side. After a while it gave up and sailed away.

Days passed. Weeks. In the brief pale nights, Vinnie dreamed and lost the dreams on waking. She longed to return to the dream room with its walls of wood and rafters and windows, with its sweet steam rising, and the laughter. To recover it, she tried to recapture the taste of maple sugar and the scent of evergreens. She tried to coax it into being with words: *America. Brooksville. Granny. Home.* But it was no use. It wouldn't come to her like a story she had memorized.

And gradually she began to understand that when Mr. Powdermaker revealed her mother's secret, he merely opened the door of a room she already lived in. That was something to think about, hard and wonderful. It wasn't the dream she sought but the thing itself. The way to it was inside, deep inside her.

A little girl not yet three, Mr. Powdermaker had said of her. Looking at Gillie and Nell made her redouble her efforts to help them know themselves. She recited nursery rhymes they might happen to recall. She sang songs and hymns that might yet remind them of the world they had left. She felt hopeful when Nell began to respond, even to ask for certain songs; but the child turned as well to village doings.

Thora came from the island, her face sunburned, her eyes full of laughter, her hair stuck with feathers. She couldn't understand why Vinnie had stayed back. Next they would be rounding up the sheep and taking the wool. Vinnie knew that meant they would be with Peg. Would Peg be expecting Vinnie to come with Thora? What could Peg know of this vigil?

To fight her longing and loneliness, Vinnie resorted to more rehearsing. Day after day the children filed down to the beach. There she rewarded them with games and stories. She sang to them at bedtime, and surprised them with fresh cheese at breakfast, a gift from Peg's parents-in-law, probably from Peg herself.

If only Vinnie could leave some gift in return. And then she thought of the rosemary growing behind the manse. She had to use a stone to dig it up. Lifting the plant with its woody root, she carried it into the graveyard and set it in the earth among the nine small stones for Peg's children. She had to clear away a tangle of weeds so that the rosemary would stand out. Even if Peg never learned that it meant remembrance, she would sense what she needed to know of it. The rosemary would thrive, and Peg would understand. Looking down at it, Vinnie began to understand too. They had had their leave-taking there in the vale, with Grace and Joel dancing circles around Peg and with Vinnie shouting her love.

Closing the graveyard gate behind her, Vinnie looked up toward the village. Everyone seemed to be gathering there. It must

179

be a special occasion, something to celebrate. Walking up to the street, she tried to get Joel's grandpapa to explain. He made a sweeping gesture that seemed to include the whole sky. Puzzled, she asked Thora, who gave her a kind of answer: the Day. The Day of days.

Vinnie thought the little ones might pick up something more, but all they knew was that there was to be a big fire. They ran back and forth carrying driftwood for the great pile growing on the hill above the village. Vinnie was staring at it, bemused, when the islanders fell still. They shaded their eyes and gazed out to the bay where a steam packet chugged into view. Some of them pointed at the plume of black smoke that billowed up. Several men shouted.

It began to dawn on Vinnie that they feared the boat was burning, for its decks were jammed with people. The island oarsmen started down the path.

As the packet pulled in, Vinnie could see that the passengers were waving. Some held up handkerchiefs that whipped about over their heads, but they didn't seem to be waving in distress. There were ladies in summer frocks and capes, some with bonnets, some wearing hats with fluttering ribbons. There were men in short coats and straw hats. They pressed against a deck rail that shone like gold. And there was something else golden behind them on a sort of raised platform. All that brightness was dazzling.

For a moment Vinnie stood rapt, as struck as the villagers. "Joel!" she shouted. It was like breaking out of a trance. "Nell! Sue-Lou! Gillie! Jamie! In line, in line!"

They came from every direction, Gillie with a stick of wood still in his hand, Nell and Sue-Lou gravitating toward each other before taking their places. They were just setting forth, Kep bounding ahead of them, when there came from the packet a rumble that turned thunderous and exploded in a brassy fanfare. The oarsmen stopped short, then scrambled back uphill. The islanders in the village gasped and ducked inside cottages or scrambled around behind. In an instant the street was almost empty.

Sue-Lou tried to break away too. "Hold her!" Vinnie shouted. She saw that Jamie had already vanished. She needed to get the children moving before she lost any more of them. "Off you go!" she yelled.

Joel said, "But Jamie's not here."

"Lead the way. I'll catch up." Vinnie ran the length of the street. Not one face showed in any doorway. Seafowl, screaming their alarm, filled the air. She called to Jamie once, and then spoke into his cottage, "Take care of him," and raced after the children.

The retreating oarsmen, colliding with each other in their haste, nearly ran full tilt into the children on the path. The wind carried the music straight to them, drums pounding, trumpets blaring.

"It's the *Argo*! It is!" Joel called back to her.

She nodded. She knew now what day this was: Midsummer. Mr. Powdermaker had kept his word.

She ran to catch up with them, meaning to take Jamie's place beside Gillie. She was almost there, almost ready to swoop down and grab Gillie's hand, when he began to swing it forward and back to the beat of the band. She saw him lift the stick of wood onto his shoulder. Was he copying someone? She glanced ahead, but Joel in the lead wasn't playing soldier. And the little ones between them were simply trotting to keep up with him.

But Gillie's steps were measured, as if somewhere inside his body a small motor had suddenly come unstuck. Up went his knees, higher and higher, and down came his bare feet—one, two, one, two—with all the solidity of boots.

When the anchor was dropped, the packet swung around. The gentlemen and ladies surged to the opposite railing, handkerchiefs flying off in the wind, cameras brought out and then shielded from the spray.

Once the children were on the beach, they acted a little scared.

181

Nell and Sue-Lou glanced back anxiously. Vinnie nodded to them. They were doing fine.

People were trying to take pictures of them. Vinnie laughed. The tourists thought Joel and Nell and Sue-Lou and Gillie were islanders. They thought *she* was an islander.

Her hand flew to her waistband; she felt the oilskin packet. The music crashed and soared. The bedraggled children spread out now, eyes on the band, on the scarlet coats and caps with gold braid. Gillie kept right on marching—one, two, one, two—like a toy soldier. She wanted to hug him. She wanted to dance and sing and turn cartwheels on the strand.

"Wave to them," she shouted, for now it was clear that the passengers were shouting greetings. They had not mistaken her and the little ones for islanders. They were cheering for the found children.

One of the men on deck lunged out to grab a lady's hat, as the wind snatched it from her head. He nearly fell over the rail. Everyone laughed at that, while the hat sailed forth, ribbons streaming as it spun and spun away.

The hat sailed shoreward. Vinnie's hands opened; her arms stretched out. She ran as the wind flung it toward her.

The children ran too. Here was the best beach game of all, and with a prize for the victor, a crown with ribbons and flowers wreathed around it.

The hat dipped. Vinnie let her hands fall. Joel, nearly catching it, shrieked with glee. But then the hat swung high on an updraft, and Vinnie gave chase again. The sun was blinding. She could feel the ribbons, her fingers closing on them, tugging, as the hat fell from the sky.

The children surrounded her, jumping up and down, clamoring for it. But she held it out of reach. Then in triumph, before the brass band and the wheeling birds and the laughing children and the cheering tourists, she brought it down and planted it firmly on her own head.

AUTHOR'S NOTE

This fiction is based on a good many historical facts. In Massachusetts in 1855 a number of immigrants were deported as paupers, among them a young woman and her infant daughter, who was an American citizen. About this time, boys from Ragged Schools for the Destitute and Delinquent Poor began to be shipped off to America as cheap labor. Within the next decade, reformers started to organize more orderly and responsible systems for assisted emigration of children. Even so, children suffered through the miserable steerage conditions on most ships and were exploited upon arrival in North America. And there were many shipwrecks, many lives lost. In 1868 an emigrant ship foundered on the rocks off the lonely Fair Isle. The passengers rescued by the islanders had to remain through the winter and be fed and clothed and sheltered. By the time they were finally taken off the island, its fragile economy was so stressed that the little island community was nearly ruined. On the even more isolated island of Saint Kilda, the native population was dying out because of a form of tetanus that killed almost every infant within the first eight days of its life. Well-intentioned efforts to improve island conditions, as well as tourism, undermined the traditional way of life and eventually led to evacuation. Some of these circumstances appear in this book on the imaginary island of Skellay.

ABOUT THE AUTHOR

BETTY LEVIN lives in Lincoln, Massachusetts, where she divides her time between sheep farming, teaching, and writing. Sheep farming includes the training and raising of working sheepdogs. Ms. Levin teaches at the Center for the Study of Children's Literature at Simmons College in Boston. This is her ninth novel for young people; her previous novel for Lodestar is *A Binding Spell*. The author is married and has three daughters.